Does Glory have what it takes to be a champion?

The colt jumped out eagerly—almost too eagerly. Cindy had to struggle to hold him to a moderate pace. Her arm muscles quivered with the effort needed to stop him from flattening out into a full gallop. Even with the firm pressure she was putting on the reins, Cindy knew they were going faster than she wanted.

Her hands and arms were trembling as she continued trying to hold Glory to a moderate pace. She felt an instant's fear that she wouldn't be able to control him. In the next split second, she pushed the fear aside. Glory wasn't deliberately disobeying his rider. He just wanted to run . . . and run. This was what he loved.

Collect all the books in
the THOROUGHBRED series:

Throughbred Super Editions

Also by Joanna Campbell:

ATTENTION: ORGANIZATIONS AND CORPORATIONS

Most HarperPaperbacks are available at special quantity discounts
for bulk purchases for sales promotions, premiums, or fund-raising.
For information, please call or write:

**Special Markets Department, HarperCollins Publishers,
10 East 53rd Street, New York, N.Y. 10022
Telephone: (212) 207-7528. Fax: (212) 207-7222.**

THOROUGHBRED

CINDY'S GLORY

JOANNA CAMPBELL

HarperPaperbacks

A Division of HarperCollins*Publishers*

If you purchased this book without a cover, you should be aware that this book is stolen property. It was reported as "unsold and destroyed" to the publisher and neither the author nor the publisher has received any payment for this "stripped book."

This is a work of fiction. The characters, incidents, and dialogues are products of the author's imagination and are not to be construed as real. Any resemblance to actual events or persons, living or dead, is entirely coincidental.

HarperPaperbacks   *A Division of* HarperCollins*Publishers*
10 East 53rd Street, New York, N.Y. 10022

Copyright © 1995 by Daniel Weiss Associates, Inc.,
and Joanna Campbell
Cover art copyright © 1995 Daniel Weiss Associates, Inc.

All rights reserved. No part of this book may be used or reproduced in any manner whatsoever without written permission of the publisher, except in the case of brief quotations embodied in critical articles and reviews. For information address Daniel Weiss Associates, Inc.,
33 West 17th Street, New York, New York 10011.

First printing: November 1995

Printed in the United States of America

HarperPaperbacks and colophon are trademarks of
HarperCollins*Publishers*

❖ 10 9 8 7 6 5 4 3 2 1

"I'll see you later, Glory," Cindy Blake murmured. "Wish us luck."

The big gray Thoroughbred colt, Glory, ducked his head and affectionately nuzzled Cindy's shining blond hair. He huffed out a soft, sweet-scented breath. Cindy gave his ears another scratch, knowing he loved it. She marveled again at the trusting kindness in his dark brown eyes. Not long before, he had been a very different horse—not trusting at all. What a difference a month had made, Cindy thought, continuing to rub Glory's ears.

Late that summer, when Cindy had discovered Glory in a paddock at a neighboring farm, she had been appalled at the cruel treatment he was receiving. Two men were rough handling him, yelling and smacking him with a whip when he didn't do what they wanted. The colt had been terrified. But from the instant she had laid eyes on him, Cindy had been awed by the colt's beauty and his courage. All she wanted to do was take him away.

Although she went to visit as often as she could, hiding in the woods next to his paddock, there was nothing Cindy could do to help the colt. She was terrified of the men herself. They'd seen her once and angrily chased her away.

Then Glory had jumped the fence and escaped onto Whitebrook land. When Cindy had found him, she hadn't known what to do. She was afraid to tell anyone at Whitebrook; then they would have to send Glory back to his owners. In desperation, she had hidden him in a feed storage shed near the back of the Whitebrook property, knowing that what she was doing was wrong—but she couldn't bear to think of the colt being sent back to more abuse. She knew what abuse was. She'd experienced plenty of it before she had come to Whitebrook.

Cindy had figured that eventually Glory's hiding place would be discovered, but when it was, no one at Whitebrook had been angry with her. Instead they began to believe her stories of his abuse. When they contacted the authorities, they discovered the colt was stolen. The neighbors had been arrested, but the authorities still hadn't tracked down Glory's rightful owner.

Until they did, Cindy had Glory to herself, but she knew in her heart that it couldn't last forever.

She leaned forward and dropped a soft kiss on Glory's muzzle, feeling her heart swell with love for the colt. She heard someone calling her from outside. "I've got to go," she told him. "We're off to the races. If Shining wins, I'll give you an extraspecial treat tonight."

The colt nickered, and Cindy let herself out of his stall and hurried toward the stable yard.

The seven entrants in the eighth and feature race at the Keeneland racetrack had just been saddled for the grade-one Queen Elizabeth II Challenge Cup. Now they gracefully paraded around the walking ring at the track in Lexington, Kentucky, their coats shimmering in the late October sunlight. All were sleek and well-conditioned three-year-old Thoroughbred fillies. But Cindy, who stood by the rail with her friends Heather Gilbert and Mandy Jarvis, had eyes only for the red roan filly wearing the number-four saddlecloth—Shining.

Cindy turned to her friends. "Shining looks gorgeous, doesn't she?"

Heather agreed with a nod and a sigh.

"Look at the way she holds up her head—like a queen!" Mandy said, inching closer to the walking ring fence on her crutches. The eight-year-old black girl had been severely injured in an automobile accident and needed partial leg braces for support, but her disability didn't dim her optimistic outlook and bubbly nature.

"She definitely is the best!" Heather's eyes sparkled. She and Cindy were both eleven years old and classmates at Henry Clay Middle School. "And Shining won't be racing against Her Majesty this time."

Her Majesty, a three-year-old filly owned by Lavinia Townsend of a rival breeding farm, Townsend Acres, had been Shining's main competition that year. To Cindy, their rivalry had caused unbelievable tension and animosity between Lavinia and Shining's owner and trainer, Samantha McLean, Cindy's soon-to-be stepsister. "I think that's why Sammy decided to enter Shining in this race," Cindy explained. "It's a turf race, and Her Majesty only races on dirt. Sammy knew Lavinia and Brad would never consider this race. I'm glad they won't be around—I get the creeps just thinking about them!"

"I don't blame you, after what Lavinia did to you!" Heather said indignantly. "I can't believe she never apologized for accusing you of stealing her stupid watch and getting you into so much trouble."

Cindy frowned. "What can you expect from Lavinia? She'd never admit she was wrong. At least they found out her watch was never stolen at all and that I was telling the truth. That sourpuss social worker Mrs. Lovell can't stop the McLeans from adopting me now."

"I'd still be mad as heck at Lavinia—especially when she hasn't even got the decency to thank you for saving her life," Heather insisted. "If you hadn't caught that runaway horse—which she shouldn't have been riding in the first place—and pulled it away from her, she would have been trampled to death."

"I am still angry," Cindy said, "but it doesn't do much good to think about it. And Brad thanked me."

"I suppose that's something," Heather conceded

4

sourly. "And now that Lavinia is expecting a baby, maybe she'll be too busy to start any more trouble."

"Let's talk about something else," Cindy said, looking across the walking ring to Shining and red-haired Samantha McLean. Cindy pushed a gleaming strand of blond hair behind her ear as she studied them. Six months ago, she hadn't known either Samantha or Shining, or Heather and Mandy, for that matter. Cindy had never set foot on Whitebrook until that desperate day when she had run away from a foster home that had become intolerable. She remembered so clearly the night she'd slipped into one of the barns at Whitebrook, seeking refuge. She'd felt so exhausted, so frightened, and so alone. In one of the stalls, Cindy had discovered two young foals, orphans like herself. Not knowing where else to go, she had curled up on the straw beside them. She would leave the barn early, she had told herself before she closed her eyes and fell into a deep sleep. But later that night Samantha had found her.

To Cindy's amazement, the McLeans had welcomed her into their home and treated her with a kindness she had never known. It was unbelievable how much her life changed in the months that followed. Sometimes she wondered if it were all a dream.

Cindy brought her thoughts back to the present and glanced around at the crowd encircling the ring. She saw that Shining was receiving other admiring glances. The filly wasn't especially big, only a little over fifteen hands, but she had beautiful conformation—long, straight legs, wide chest, strong hindquarters, and an

5

elegant head with wide-set, intelligent eyes. Her roan coloring was eye-catching, too, her red-flecked coat set off by black legs, mane, and tail.

"So Sammy thinks Shining's going to be as good on the grass as she is on the dirt?" Heather asked.

"Sammy thinks Shining can handle the grass even better than the dirt," Cindy answered. "Sammy's been working her on the turf course at Whitebrook the last couple of weeks. And Sammy wouldn't have entered Shining in this race if she thought Shining would have a problem."

Heather nudged Cindy with her elbow. "Look at that number-three horse, the dark bay." Heather looked down at the program in her hands. "Grecian Delight," she murmured. "She's won the last three times out."

"I know," Cindy said, "but not against this kind of competition. Shining outclasses her."

Mandy grinned. "She's classy, all right, but I remember how awful she looked when she first came to Whitebrook—her coat all shaggy and her bones sticking out."

Cindy hadn't known Shining then, but looking at the beautiful red roan filly now, she found it hard to believe Shining had ever been in such sad shape. As she circled the ring, Shining's ears were pricked, and she gazed with interest at the crowd gathered around the ring. There was a spring in her step, and her muscles rippled powerfully under her sleek coat. The filly seemed to know she looked good—better than the other six fillies in the field.

"Wouldn't it be something if you could watch Glory race someday," Heather said with a touch of awe in her voice.

"I think about it all the time," Cindy murmured, her thoughts going to the magnificent gray colt at Whitebrook.

"Here come the jockeys," Mandy cried, dark eyes alight. "There's Ashleigh."

They all watched as the brightly silked jockeys entered the walking ring and went to their respective mounts. Ashleigh Griffen, whose husband, Mike Reese, and his father, Gene, owned Whitebrook with her, looked slim and professional in Mike's blue-and-white silks. She smiled at Samantha as she stopped at Shining's side. Ashleigh was in her early twenties, but had been riding professionally since she was sixteen and had trained her beloved mare, Wonder, to become a champion. Wonder was retired now at Whitebrook, but her offspring were doing just as well, as was Wonder's half-sister, Shining.

"Ashleigh doesn't look worried," Heather said as the trim jockey settled in Shining's saddle, gathered the reins, and listened to Samantha's instructions. Together they had trained Shining, and Ashleigh had ridden the filly in all her races.

"Someday I want to ride like Ashleigh," Mandy said with a sigh.

"You will," Cindy told the younger girl, wishing with all her heart that were true, but there were no guarantees that Mandy would ever recover full use of her legs. "They're ready to go out to the track," she added a moment later. "We'd better go to our seats." The three made their way to the grandstand at a slow pace so that Mandy could keep up. At the foot of the stairs Cindy's new foster father, Ian McLean, caught up with them and smiled. "Ready for the race? How about a lift, Mandy?"

He swooped the younger girl up in his arms and carried her to their reserved seats. Tor Nelson, Samantha's longtime boyfriend, had just arrived. Cindy spotted his blond head as he waved to them. Tor and his father owned a riding stable in Lexington, and Tor was a top-class show-jump rider. "What a crowd!" Tor said as they slid into their seats.

"The weather doesn't hurt," Mr. McLean replied. "This is what I'd call a perfect October day."

Cindy glanced around at the packed grandstand, the clear blue sky overhead, the very green grass of the turf course and infield, and beyond, to the brilliant splash of fall color on the trees. Keeneland was a beautiful track, but it would seem even more beautiful to Cindy if Shining won today.

Samantha arrived, looking both nervous and excited, and sat down next to Tor as the horses came onto the track for the post parade. *I'd be nervous too*, Cindy thought, *if a horse I owned and trained were racing*.

Cindy's eyes were glued to Shining and Ashleigh as their escort rider led them past the stands. They were fourth in the seven-horse field. Shining tossed her elegant head and pranced a few steps as if to say, "Look at me. I'm going to win!" Cindy smiled and crossed her fingers. She wasn't really superstitious, but crossing her fingers wouldn't hurt, she figured.

The field paraded past the stands, then turned to begin their warm-up jog toward the starting gate. The grade-one race was a mile and an eighth over the inner turf course. All the three-year-old fillies entered had proven themselves in previous races. All of them, except Shining, had raced and won on the grass before.

Cindy felt a small twinge of uncertainty but quickly pushed it away. She had complete faith in Samantha and Shining, and if Samantha thought the filly was ready to race on the grass, then she was. Cindy had always felt a bond with Shining. They had so much in common. They'd both been mistreated and distrustful of others, and neither of them had known love until they had come to Whitebrook. But both of them had the instinct to survive and do better.

Cindy focused all her thoughts on the track as the seven fillies began loading into the gate. The first three went in smoothly, then Shining and the number-five horse, but the next horse refused to go in. Tense seconds passed as the gate attendants first tried to lead the filly in, then pushed her, then finally resorted to blindfolding her. Only then did she reluctantly go into the gate, but the horses already loaded had had extra moments to fidget and lose their concentration. Cindy focused her binoculars on Shining but couldn't see clearly whether the filly was alert. The last horse loaded, the gate doors flew open, and the race was off!

9

Six powerful Thoroughbreds jumped out onto the track, but Cindy cringed to see that Shining was off half a stride slow. The filly couldn't have been concentrating when the gates opened. She had jumped out too late. But Cindy could see, too, that Ashleigh had immediately gotten Shining's attention, and as the field headed past the stands for the first time, Shining was starting to dig in.

"She's last," Mandy said mournfully.

"It's too soon to worry," Cindy told her. "She'll make it up." Cindy only hoped she was right, because as the field streamed over the course and spread out along the rail, Shining was at least eight lengths behind the leader. And Shining liked to run on or close to the lead.

Shining was gradually eating into the lead, though, as the field went into the clubhouse turn. She edged past one filly, then another. Cindy could almost feel Shining's determination to outrun her rivals.

Slowly, as the field moved up the backstretch, Shining continued to gain. Cindy was barely aware of her cries of encouragement. "Go, girl! Go! Show them!" From the corner of her eye she saw Samantha, Ian McLean, and Tor leaning forward in their seats. Cindy gripped the grandstand rail in front of her.

Shining was four wide as the field came around the far turn, but there was only one horse in front of her now. Ashleigh moved Shining in closer to the rail and went in hot pursuit. Shining's strides lengthened; she found another gear and powered up toward the lead horse. She started moving up alongside.

10

"Go, Shining! Come on, girl! We love you!" Cindy screeched.

"And down the stretch they come," the announcer cried. "Grecian Delight holding on to a short lead, but Shining is moving up fast along her outside. At the eighth pole, they're neck and neck."

Cindy thought of Glory, wondering if one day she would see the beautiful gray colt racing toward the finish line, overpowering all his rivals. Her heart fluttered with excitement at the thought, then sank as she realized that Glory might not even stay at Whitebrook if the Jockey Club tracked down his real owner and the owner wanted him back. His future was completely uncertain.

The announcer's excited voice broke into her thoughts. "Shining has taken the lead!" he cried. "With less than an eighth to go, Shining takes control! She's sprinting away from the rest of the field . . . by a length, a length and a half—" The announcer's voice caught.

So did Cindy's when she saw Ashleigh suddenly wobble in the saddle. She heard her foster father groan, and Samantha give a yelp of dismay.

"Ashleigh Griffen's lost a stirrup!" the announcer shouted. "What a terrible twist of fate. Can she hold on to the finish? Grecian Delight is gaining on the inside. . . . "

Cindy knew how difficult and dangerous the ride had become for Ashleigh. With only one stirrup, her balance would be thrown off. She would have difficulty holding her body over Shining's withers—and if she fell now, with six powerful Thoroughbreds bearing down on her at a full gallop . . . Cindy swallowed.

Yet Ashleigh was managing to hang on, and despite an unbalanced rider in her saddle, Shining was determined. On her own she dug in again and sprinted toward the wire. Ashleigh had wrapped her fingers in Shining's mane; she'd pressed her stirrupless leg against Shining's side, desperately trying to stay in the saddle.

Cindy felt her heart pound with fear and excitement. "Hold on, Ashleigh! Hold on!" If only Ashleigh could manage to keep her seat until they passed the finish. Cindy stopped breathing as they powered the last strides to the wire. She felt as though she were watching Shining and Ashleigh in slow motion. Never had the last few yards of a race seemed to take so long. Of course, she knew it wasn't taking long at all—Shining was flying!

Cindy jumped to her feet, her hands still gripping the railing in front of her. Unconsciously she leaned forward, her eyes on the wire. Ashleigh and Shining swept under it. Cindy let out her breath in a whoosh. They'd won! Shining and Ashleigh had won!

"They did it!" she screamed, hugging Mandy and Heather and then Samantha, who was beaming.

"Amazing! What a ride!" Samantha cried. The announcer seemed to feel the same. "Shining takes the Queen Elizabeth II Challenge Cup despite a broken stirrup—an incredible ride by Ashleigh Griffen! Grecian Delight in second, Capricole a distant third . . . but wait! Griffen has been unseated!"

Cindy looked up the track where the riders of the other horses were slowing their mounts. Ashleigh was flat on her back on the ground, and Shining was galloping riderless up the track. Samantha and Tor were already rushing down the stairs toward the track. Ashleigh and Shining had definitely won, since they'd crossed the finish with Ashleigh still in the saddle, but the broken stirrup must have finally taken its toll on Ashleigh. She must have lost her balance trying to slow Shining down.

The other jockeys reined their now cantering mounts around the fallen jockey, then quickly turned them and rode back toward Ashleigh, who still lay immobile on the grass. One of the riders dismounted and came to Ashleigh's aid. The other jockeys and horses blocked Cindy's view.

Ashleigh's hurt! Cindy thought in panic. Several seconds passed as she stood frozen in dread. Then one of the jockeys moved to the side, and Cindy had a clear view of Ashleigh again.

Ashleigh had lifted herself up on one elbow, and as Cindy watched, Ashleigh, with one of the other jockeys' help, slowly began to rise. A cheer went up from the crowd. Cindy's knees nearly buckled in relief. But what about Shining? Cindy's eyes swept up the track, searching for Shining. An escort rider was heading the filly off far up the track, but Shining had already slowed down on her own. The escort rider rode up beside the filly and reached out to take her reins and lead her back.

Cindy and the others rushed after Samantha and Tor down the grandstand steps and pushed through the crowd. When they reached the track side, Ashleigh was walking off the inner turf course toward them. Her silks were grass, stained, but she was grinning from ear to ear. Samantha hurried out to meet her. They spoke quickly, then hugged and waited as the escort rider brought Shining to them.

The crowd was already thick around the winner's circle as Samantha, Ashleigh, and Shining entered. The fans loudly cheered Ashleigh again, and she smiled and waved to them in thanks.

Cindy realized she was trembling.

"It's a good thing she held on until the race was over," Heather murmured. She didn't need to say more. They all knew how easily Ashleigh could have been trampled and seriously hurt.

Mr. McLean shepherded the girls into the winner's circle as Ashleigh removed Shining's saddle to weigh in. "I'm fine," Ashleigh replied to their worried questions. "A little bruised, but fine." She gave a brilliant smile. "I can't complain after that kind of a win. Shining saved the day."

"I don't know how that leather could have broken," Samantha said worriedly to her father. "I checked over all the equipment. Thank God neither of them was hurt."

"These things happen," Mr. McLean said quietly. "Don't blame yourself. I'm sure Ashleigh doesn't blame you."

"No," Samantha agreed. "But it still upsets me." She glanced toward Cindy, Heather, and Mandy, and her expression lightened. "Come on. I can see you guys are dying to congratulate Shining."

Cindy hurried forward to hug Shining's gleaming

neck. "You did an incredible job, like you always do," Cindy cried. "We're all proud of you."

Shining softly huffed her appreciation and rubbed her head gently against Cindy's arm. By the time Heather and Mandy had added their praise, Ashleigh returned. Samantha strapped another saddle on Shining's steaming back, and Ashleigh mounted for the winner's photo. Shining arched her neck proudly for the photo, and the crowd again roared their approval.

Before dismounting, Ashleigh leaned over and whispered to Samantha, "I left the damaged saddle with the stewards. I'll meet you on the backside after I change."

Cindy saw Samantha's grim nod and suddenly had a horrible thought. Had the saddle been tampered with? Was the broken stirrup leather not an accident after all?

As quickly as the thought entered her mind, she shook it away. If Lavinia or Brad Townsend had been at the track, she would have reason to be suspicious, but she couldn't imagine anyone else who would sabotage Shining or endanger Ashleigh. *No, it was just an accident*, she told herself.

2

IT WAS DARK BY THE TIME THEY RETURNED TO WHITEBROOK, on the outskirts of Lexington, with the victorious Shining. Shining had come out of the race in incredible shape, despite her slow start and Ashleigh's imbalance after the unexpected breakage of the stirrup leather. On the backside after the race, while Cindy had helped bathe and cool Shining, she'd listened carefully to what Samantha and Ashleigh had to say about the race. Samantha had collected the saddle and examined it with her father and Ashleigh.

The leather had detached at the point where it was stitched to the saddle. The stitching had ripped. Samantha could only conclude that the break was due to flawed workmanship. There was no reason to suspect it was anything but an accident.

Mike and Gene Reese, Whitebrook's trusted black stable manager, Len, and their full-time groom, Vic, came out to meet the van as Ian McLean parked it in the drive. They were all smiling and called their congratulations to Samantha as she jumped down from the double cab. Ashleigh followed, and Mike gave her a tight hug. Ashleigh had already called Mike from the track, knowing he'd be worried after her fall.

"You nearly scared me to death, but that was some incredible riding, Ash!" he said proudly.

Ashleigh smiled up at him. "I was pretty scared myself when the stirrup gave way, but it turned out fine in the end."

"I'll say," Len said as he went to help Samantha unload Shining from the van. "She sure showed them her stuff today."

Cindy and Heather, who was spending the night, climbed down from the van, too. After Samantha had carefully checked Shining over, Len led the filly off for a well-deserved rest in her stall.

"Let's go see Glory," Cindy said to Heather as the others remained in the stable yard talking about the race.

Heather nodded eagerly, and they hurried into the training barn, where Len had just led Shining. There were three barns on the Whitebrook property—the mares and foals' barn, the training barn, and a smaller stallion barn behind. All the exercise horses and active racehorses were stabled in the training barn. Glory's stall was near the end of the long aisle.

Elegant Thoroughbreds stuck their heads over their stall doors and nickered as Cindy and Heather passed. Len was in Shining's stall, removing her leg wraps. He grinned and winked when he saw the girls. "I can guess where you're going," he called. "Don't worry. He's just fine. I checked on him an hour ago. A couple of the cats were keeping him company."

"Thanks, Len." Cindy and Heather hurried on eagerly. Glory had heard Cindy's voice, and he thrust his gray head over the stall door and whickered a greeting.

"Hi, big guy!" Cindy called. "Did you miss me? We had a great day. Shining won! All I could think of was you being on the track one day."

Cindy kissed Glory's velvety muzzle, then unbolted the stall door. She and Heather stepped inside. Two stable cats rose from where they'd been lying on the stall partition and stretched. The bigger cat was named Jeeves because his shiny black coat had white markings that resembled a butler's white collar and cuffs. The younger cat, whom Cindy had named Imp, was still a kitten and had kept Glory company during the days Cindy had hidden Glory in the shed. He had unusual gray calico coloring that nearly matched the dappled gray of Glory's coat.

Glory nudged Cindy happily. She reached up to scratch his ears. "I'll bet you're waiting for a treat," she said, then dug in her pocket and pulled out a carrot. She broke it in half and fed it to the colt. He quickly lipped it up and munched with pleasure.

Imp gracefully jumped down from the stall partition to land in the middle of Glory's back. The colt barely reacted, except for cocking an ear back in Imp's

18

direction. In the short time he'd been at Whitebrook, Glory had grown accustomed to one cat or another curling up on his back and seemed to enjoy it. Imp sat down and studiously began grooming himself, licking the side of his front paw and scrubbing it over his face.

Heather chuckled. "It's so neat how they get along. I wish I could have a cat, but our dog would be jealous. He's almost twelve—like me—and my mom says he's too old to accept another animal in the house."

"Well, you can play with the cats when you come over here. Len told me he thinks Snowshoe is going to have another litter. He's decided to have her fixed. Otherwise, pretty soon there will be more cats than horses here."

They both laughed. Cindy fed Glory the rest of the carrot. "Ah-ah . . . no more," she said when he sniffed her pocket for another. "You'll get spoiled. I'll bring you some more in the morning when I come to groom you and take you out."

Cindy rubbed the colt's silky neck.

"I know what you were thinking during the race today," Heather said quietly. "You were thinking of Glory racing."

Cindy nodded. "It would be so great if he could stay here and we could train him. I know he's got talent— well, actually, I don't know enough about training racehorses yet to be sure, but I believe it inside."

"Like Sammy believed in Shining when she first came here. No one else thought Shining would ever race again."

"Just like that," Cindy agreed, letting her gaze rest on Glory. He was tall, just over sixteen hands, with an elegant head and wide-set eyes. His legs were straight and strong, and his muscles rippled under his coat, even though almost the only exercise he'd had in the last month had been walks and a romp in the paddock. "I can just picture him in the winner's circle, and all I can think is that if he didn't have the potential to be a good racehorse, why would those men have stolen him?"

Heather agreed. "I know. It wouldn't make sense for them to steal a loser, but I can't understand why the Jockey Club hasn't found his real owner yet. His lip is tattooed, so he must have been registered."

"But his tattoo was changed, remember? The horse registered under Glory's tattoo was named Parkway Runner, but they know it was a different horse because the blood types don't match." Cindy wagged her head. "Anyway, I hope they never find the real owner. Then I'd lose Glory—they'd take him back. I couldn't stand it!"

Heather was thoughtful for a moment. "Have you ever talked to Sammy about training Glory . . . or putting him back in training? From what we saw when he was at the neighbors', he'd had some training, and Mike said that those crooks were planning to race him."

"I haven't said anything to Sammy," Cindy replied. "I kind of know what she'd say, or Mike and my foster father would say. We don't own Glory. He's only staying here until his owner is found."

"But you've been riding him," Heather said.

Cindy smiled to herself. "Yes. I rode him on the lanes this week. Sammy was with me. We never went faster than a trot, but he felt so powerful and smooth. He hasn't forgotten how those men abused him, though, and he won't let anyone on his back except me. How can Sammy, or Mike, or my foster father find out if he's good or bad if they can't ride him? No one's going to listen to me. I don't know enough."

"Maybe his real owner won't want him," Heather said hopefully. "Then he can stay here and start trusting people again. Then someone else could ride him and see how good he is. The McLeans are adopting you. You can practice and get good enough at riding and training so you could ride him yourself!"

Cindy wished that with all her heart, but she knew only too well how life could disappoint. In her brief eleven and a half years, she had spent time in six different foster homes, each one worse than the next. Until she'd come to Whitebrook, she'd never known happiness, but she still didn't believe in miracles.

She gave Glory a last pat. "We'll be back to see you later, gorgeous," she said.

Glory nickered softly, then Cindy and Heather left the stall and returned to the stable yard.

The others were still there, but Cindy's foster mother, Beth McLean, had joined them. Beth had married Ian McLean that summer, after Cindy arrived at Whitebrook, and the two of them were blissfully happy. Ian McLean's first wife, Samantha's mother, had died in a riding accident about six years before, when Samantha

21

was twelve. Cindy knew that Ian and Beth had moved up their wedding date so that they could provide a stable home environment for her and thwart the social workers who wanted to send her to yet another foster home. But from what Cindy could judge, Beth and Samantha got along great.

Beth's blond curls shimmered in the barn spotlight as she greeted Cindy and Heather. "So, what did you think of the big race?" she asked.

"Amazing," Heather said. "I don't think I could have stayed in the saddle like Ashleigh did. I'm so glad I met Cindy and have a chance to see this farm and the track!"

Beth looked to Cindy, whose eyes were sparkling. "You know I loved it," Cindy said. "Shining and Ashleigh were incredible!"

Beth smiled. "I thought that might be your reaction, but enough of standing out here and talking about the race. I've got a big dinner ready in the house. I figured you'd all be starving."

"We are!" Samantha said with a laugh. "I was so excited after the race, I didn't even think of getting anything to eat at the track."

"Well, the food's ready whenever you all are. Ashleigh, Mike, Gene, I hope you'll join us. Where's Tor, Sammy?" Beth asked.

"He's stopping at his stable to see if everything's all right. He'll be here in a minute."

"We still have to check the horses for the night," Ian said, "but I think they can wait until we've eaten."

They all followed Beth across the stable yard into the

McLeans' cottage. Next door to the cottage was the white farmhouse where Ashleigh, Mike, and Gene Reese lived. Len and Vic had another cottage behind the barns and not far from the mile training oval, where the horses in active training were worked. Beyond stretched acres of green-grassed, white-fenced paddocks, which were now lit by the silvery gleam of moonlight. Cindy loved Whitebrook. To her, it was the most wonderful place in the world.

As soon as they entered the five-room cottage, they were greeted by the luscious smells of hot food. Beth had pulled out the leaves of the kitchen table, and its surface was covered by bowls and platters. Cindy knew that everything would be delicious but healthy, since Beth was a nut about nutrition. Sure enough, there were three kinds of vegetables, steamed not boiled, a huge green salad, and one of Beth's specialties—low-fat fried chicken, floured after the skin was removed, then baked.

"Find a seat, everyone," Beth instructed, bringing a pitcher of fruit juice to the table. Chairs scraped across the floor as they eagerly took seats.

"I'm hungry enough to finish off that chicken all by myself," Ian said.

Mike chuckled. "The rest of us aren't going to give you the opportunity." He helped himself to a drumstick from the platter.

The front door opened, and Tor stepped inside. "So here you all are—and you started eating without me!" he said with mock indignation.

"We just started," Samantha called. She patted the seat next to her. "Come on. Sit down."

Tor stepped around the table. "So what did you think of the race?" he asked Mike.

Mike grinned. "Aside from a near cardiac arrest when the stirrup broke, I thought it was fantastic. I couldn't be happier for Sammy. It looks like Shining will have another good year ahead."

"I hope," Samantha said. "Whitebrook's going to have a lot of prospects next year, with Mr. Wonderful and Precocious starting their two-year-old seasons. I'm getting excited about it already."

Mike nodded. "Ian and I have a couple of other promising horses in the barn, and of course Sierra will continue steeplechasing."

As Mike spoke, Cindy gazed off into space, thinking of Glory and wishing with all her heart that he could be one of Whitebrook's promising prospects too. Heather glanced in her direction, and the two girls exchanged an understanding look.

Horse and farm talk dominated the conversation throughout the rest of the meal. They'd certainly done justice to Beth's cooking. Barely a scrap was left. "We'll help with the dishes," Cindy offered as Beth rose to start clearing.

"I'll take care of them," Beth said cheerfully. "I know you're dying to get out to see the horses. Tomorrow you guys can have dish duty."

Before everyone headed out to the barns, they carried their plates to the sink. Beth was already scraping the vegetable scraps into a bucket for her compost pile.

Once out in the stables, Heather and Cindy pitched in

24

to help with the evening chores, checking haynets and water buckets. Then they went to the feed room and filled their pockets with carrots. With the work done, they could visit Glory again, and all the rest of the special horses.

In the mares' barn they stopped at Wonder's stall. The champion chestnut mare was nearly eleven but still fit and beautiful, with a disposition to match her looks. She nickered gratefully when Cindy and Heather offered her carrots. The mare was in foal and due to give birth in the spring. Sadly, Wonder had lost her previous year's foal through miscarriage, but her yearling son, Mr. Wonderful, would be beginning his racing career that coming season. Ashleigh and Len were keeping an especially careful eye on Wonder now, and so far all looked good.

The girls gave Wonder a last pat and moved on down the row of stalls. There were two dozen in all in the mares' barn. The stalls that weren't occupied by broodmares housed the yearlings and weanlings. When the yearlings began their training after the New Year, they would be moved over into the training barn.

Their next stop was at Fleet Goddess's stall—Ashleigh's other retired race mare. Goddess was wide awake and pricked her ears as they approached. Like Wonder, she had won major races during her career, and her yearling filly, Precocious, was set to go into training with Mr. Wonderful. Goddess's foal of that year, a colt named Fleeting Moment, was stabled at the other end of the barn with the other weanlings.

Goddess stretched her nearly black head over the stall door and whuffed impatiently. Cindy smiled. "We're coming, girl. Don't worry, I haven't forgotten your bedtime snack."

They stayed with Goddess for several minutes, stroking her silky neck and scratching her ears, which she loved. Then they made their last stop at the side-by-side stalls of Mr. Wonderful and Precocious. The young horses pranced across their stalls, then nudged the girls with their noses. Precocious was the image of her sire, Mike's prize stallion, Jazzman. She was tall for a filly, and she was coal black, with a triangular white star on her forehead like her mother's.

Mr. Wonderful resembled his dam, Wonder, except that his chestnut coat was more honey-colored than Wonder's. Both of the yearlings had been broken to saddle and longe line earlier in the fall, and everyone at Whitebrook was excited about their futures.

"Sorry, don't have anything for you," Cindy teased Precocious as the filly sniffed at Cindy's pockets. "Oh, you think there's something still in there?" Both girls laughed at the filly as she tried to push her nose into Cindy's pocket, even though her muzzle was too big to fit. "Okay, you win," Cindy said with a laugh. "I saved something for you. Move your nose so I can get it."

Precocious lifted her head long enough for Cindy to pull out a carrot, then eagerly lipped it up. Heather gave Mr. Wonderful his treat. "I can't wait until they go into real training," Heather said. "It's going to be so much fun to watch."

26

"I know," Cindy agreed. "Of course, it's too soon to tell if they're going to be great racehorses."

Heather smiled confidently. "Oh, I think they will."

"Yeah, me too," Cindy said. "It's getting late. We'll just have enough time to visit Pride and Shining and say good night to Glory."

They hurried out of the mares' barn across the lane behind to the smaller stallion barn. Whitebrook was still growing, and as yet the farm only had five stallions. Jazzman and Pride were the superstars.

Pride had the first stall on the right. He was Wonder's firstborn, and if her other foals had inherited the same amount of talent, they would be stars too. Pride had been retired the year before when he'd nearly died from the aftereffects of a twisted intestine. He was healthy again now, though, and in the spring his first crop of foals would be born.

Len was in Pride's stall, checking the stallion's hay and water. He smiled when he saw Cindy and Heather. "I don't know about you girls. You're going to spoil the horses rotten with all those treats."

"No, we're not, Len," Cindy protested. "Just ask Beth—carrots are very healthy. Besides, I've seen you giving the horses extra treats too."

Len chuckled. "Caught me. Well, come on in and say good night to him. And here's Sidney."

As the girls entered the stall, a stocky white cat with black markings that resembled a mask over his face trotted in behind them. Pride lowered his head, and the two animals touched noses. Then Sidney gave a mighty

27

leap up onto Pride's back, sat down, and began to purr with a deep rumble.

"He sleeps with Pride every night," Cindy told Heather.

"And has done for a long time," Len added. "They're good company for one another."

It was almost nine when the girls revisited the training barn. They looked into Shining's stall, but the roan filly was dozing, and they didn't disturb her. After her race that day, she'd earned her rest.

They hurried on to Glory's stall. He was glad to see them and dropped his head to have his ears scratched. Cindy hugged the big gray's neck. *It's been such a perfect day*, she thought. *If only things could stay this way forever.*

3

THE PEACE AND TRANQUILLITY CINDY FELT LASTED A FEW days, then she woke, shuddering, from a terrible nightmare. Her heart was pounding and her nightgown was drenched with sweat. She drew in ragged breaths as she stared around her darkened room, not sure where she was.

The dream had seemed so real. The social workers had come to get her. They had decided that the McLeans couldn't adopt her after all, and they were taking her to another foster home far away. Mrs. Lovell had smiled with evil satisfaction as a policeman dragged Cindy from the cottage. Cindy had screamed and kicked, but they had forced her into their car. She cried out to her foster parents to help her, but they had just looked on sadly.

Then she had seen herself in a strange room, crammed in with five other girls. They were making fun of her, laughing at her. "So you thought you could get away," they jeered. "You thought you could stay with someone who loved you. Ha ha. You're an orphan. Nobody will ever love you!"

That was when she had jerked awake. Her worst nightmare had come true. Gradually her eyes adjusted to the dimness, the silence, and she realized she was alone, in her small bedroom at the McLeans'. It had once been a storage room, but Cindy didn't care. It was the first room of her own she'd ever had—except maybe in the dim past before her parents had died. She didn't remember them or what her life had been like then.

With still trembling hands, she reached for the light beside her bed and turned it on. Instantly the room was flooded with warmth. Beth and Samantha had repainted the room for her in a soft rose. Beth had found an old iron bed at a garage sale, painted it white, and made curtains and bedspread in a cheerful floral print chintz. Ashleigh's parents had given them an old desk that fit under the eves. On the walls Cindy had hung pictures of horses and the drawing of Glory that Heather had done for her. Heather was an incredible artist.

It took several minutes before Cindy's heart stopped pounding and she felt calm enough to turn off the light and go back to sleep. In the morning, though, the dream still troubled her.

Her foster parents were in the kitchen when she went down. Her foster father was swallowing down a cup of coffee.

"Good morning, Cindy," they both said brightly.

"Good morning, Beth, Ian," Cindy answered.

They had only been her foster parents for a short time—a month, actually. When the battles with the child welfare people were finally resolved and the McLeans officially became Cindy's foster parents, they'd all talked one night.

"I know that you don't know what to call us," Ian said. "You probably don't feel comfortable calling us Mom and Dad, since we're not your real parents, but Mr. and Mrs. McLean sounds too formal. How about calling us Ian and Beth?"

Cindy was grateful for his words. She honestly hadn't known what to call them. It was true, she didn't feel comfortable with Mom and Dad, but she hoped, if everything went well, they would soon be her adoptive parents. "That's okay with me," she said finally.

Ian and Beth both smiled. "Good."

"I think we'll all be more comfortable now," Beth said, taking Cindy's hand and squeezing it. "I've never liked formalities anyway. No matter what we call each other, you're one of the family, Cindy, like me. I'm pretty new, too!" Beth laughed.

Cindy had smiled, warming to them both. But today she thought of the dream she'd had, and the girls taunting her. "You're an orphan. Nobody will ever love you!"

No! It was just a dream, Cindy convinced herself as she went out to the stables. Beth and Ian cared about her, and she cared about them.

At school that day she and Heather met for lunch,

31

and Cindy told Heather about the dream. There were rowdy screams of laughter from the next table, where all the most popular kids met.

Cindy glanced over at them in irritation. She and Heather had never gotten in with the popular crowd. Heather was too shy to make overtures, and Cindy couldn't deal with a bunch of silly airheads. She knew she wasn't being fair in prejudging them, but she still was distrustful of strangers and maybe always would be.

"It was only a dream, Cindy," Heather said reassuringly when the laughter at the next table had subsided. "There isn't any reason for the Child Welfare Department to change their minds and take you away from the McLeans. They've already filed adoption papers."

Cindy nodded. "But they haven't heard anything back yet."

"It probably takes time for everything to get sorted out. My parents are always complaining about bureaucratic red tape."

Cindy smiled to hear Heather using such a grown-up expression, but she realized Heather was probably right. It was too soon to worry about the adoption not being finalized yet. "Why don't you come home on the bus with me today?" she asked her friend. "I can take Glory out, and you can ride Bo Jangles."

Heather's eyes immediately lit. "I'd love to. I'll call my mom before we go back to class."

The afternoon was slightly overcast, which made the fall foliage seem even more brilliant in contrast. The girls quickly tacked up Glory and Bo Jangles, one of Mike's exercise horses.

"You girls take it easy out there," Len called to them as they headed up one of the grassy lanes between the paddocks.

"Don't you trust us?" Cindy called back good-naturedly.

"It's not that," Len said, "but you've got a lot of horse under you. Don't let him get the upper hand."

"He'd never try to take advantage," Cindy replied, patting Glory's neck. "Would you, boy?"

Glory tossed his head as if to say he wouldn't think of it.

"Have fun, then," Len called in parting.

"You're not worried about Glory acting up, are you?" Heather asked.

"No. It's just that Sammy has always ridden out with me before. Len's just being cautious. Let's trot them." Cindy tapped Glory with her heels, and the big colt sprang forward into a trot. Heather, on Bo Jangles, followed suit.

"Glory's strides are so much longer than Bo's," Heather said. "I wonder what Glory would do at a canter."

"I haven't tried him yet." Then Cindy's eyes twinkled. "But I could today."

"Would the others get upset?" Heather asked. "You said you only walked and trotted when Sammy rode with you, and Len said to be careful."

"I'll be careful," Cindy answered quickly. "We can canter down one of the lanes. I can ride well enough now that I'm not going to fall off."

"I wasn't thinking that you'd fall. It's just that Glory doesn't belong to Whitebrook. If anything happened to him—"

"It won't," Cindy cut in. "He canters all around the paddocks."

"Yeah, you're right," Heather agreed. "And I suppose you'll never know if he's got any potential if you don't ride him faster than a trot."

"We'll trot to the end of the lane to loosen them up, then canter down one of the side lanes. Okay?"

"Sure," Heather said, warming to the idea. "But I think you'll leave us in the dust."

Cindy grinned. That was exactly what she wanted Glory to do. They were out of sight of the barns, not far from the shed where she had hidden Glory. When they reached the end of the lane, Cindy reined Glory to the right and stopped, facing up one of the grassy side lanes. Heather pulled Bo up next to them. The lane, bordered by the white fences of the neighboring paddocks, stretched straight ahead for about a quarter of a mile before ending at the edge of a meadow. Beyond the meadow was woodland, threaded with cross-country trails.

"We can canter to the end of the lane, then turn in the meadow," Cindy said. "Ready?"

Heather nodded and adjusted the chin strap of her hard hat. "Let's do it!"

Simultaneously the girls heeled their mounts forward. Glory strode out eagerly in a cantering stride. Cindy was aware of Heather and Bo beside them during the first several strides, then Glory effortlessly moved ahead. Cindy sat back, thrilling to the rocking-horse gait of the canter, listening to the rhythmic thud of Glory's hooves on the turf and the sound of his snorted breaths. The wind rushed against her cheeks, and she felt as if she were flying. If Glory could canter at this speed, what could he do at a gallop?

Halfway down the lane, she glanced back and saw Heather and Bo Jangles far behind. Her lips turned in a wide smile. Nothing she had experienced before could compare with what she was feeling. She'd been thrilled and awed when Samantha had let her ride Shining, but riding Glory was pure heaven!

Too soon they reached the end of the lane. As they entered the meadow, Cindy sat back and gently drew on the reins, circling Glory until he dropped back into a trot. Heather was just coming off the lane.

"What did I tell you?" she asked, laughing. "Bo and I didn't have a chance. Glory really is amazing. I don't think I've ever seen such a long-striding horse."

Cindy beamed at her friend and lovingly patted Glory's neck. "He's something, isn't he? And he's not even winded." Then Cindy suddenly sobered, remembering the uncertainty of Glory's future . . . of her own future, for that matter. But she wasn't going to ruin her day by thinking about that now.

"Have you been watching the morning workouts?"

Heather asked as they headed back toward the stable yard.

"Whenever I can, though there aren't that many this time of year. Only the horses that will be racing in Florida over the winter are being worked. The others are being rested."

"But have you seen enough to tell whether Glory is as good as the horses in training?"

"I think he is, or could be. Still, there's a lot more involved in training a racehorse." She wagged her head. "I can't be sure."

Heather sighed. "Well, at least you can take him out here and ride him. The more you ride him, the better both of you will get."

"If his owner doesn't take him away."

Heather didn't respond. They both knew the chances of Glory remaining indefinitely at Whitebrook were slim.

That evening after dinner, Cindy went to her room and diligently did her homework. Although she didn't find school that difficult, especially now that she was in a happy home, she was determined to get the best grades possible—straight A's, if she could manage it. She wasn't going to let anything jeopardize her adoption proceedings, and bad grades would. Early in the fall, when she'd been preoccupied with hiding Glory, she'd flunked a surprise history quiz. Mrs. Lovell had been quick to learn about the failing grade and had tried to use it as justification for taking Cindy from the McLeans. That wasn't going to happen again.

Cindy finished up her last assignment, closed her book, then leaned back in her chair. Her eyes went to Heather's drawing of Glory, and she thought about her conversation with Heather that afternoon. Could she convince her foster father to work Glory on the track—train him with the rest of the Whitebrook horses? It wouldn't cost anything extra, and she desperately wanted to prove that Glory had talent. The worst that could happen was that Ian would say no.

Still, Cindy felt a twinge of uncertainty. The McLeans had been so good to her. She didn't want to seem ungrateful by asking too much of them. Then she thought of Glory and decided that, for his sake, she at least had to ask.

She left her bedroom and went downstairs. Samantha was out with Tor, but Ian and Beth were in the living room. Beth was curled up in a chair, reading, and Ian was working on some accounts. They both looked up and smiled as she entered the room.

"Finished your homework?" Beth asked pleasantly.

Cindy nodded.

"Turn on the TV if you want," Ian said. "It won't bother us."

Cindy swallowed. "I wanted to ask you something."

Her foster father leaned back in his chair. "Sure. Shoot."

"It's about Glory. I . . . I wanted to know if you'd let him train with your other horses," she finished in a rush. "I know he's not ours, but he's got so much talent, and he's been through so much. If you would put him in training, you could see how good he is . . ." Her voice trailed off when she saw her foster father's expression.

"Cindy, I know how attached you are to that colt, but you have to be realistic. The Jockey Club will trace his rightful owner. It's not a matter of 'if,' but 'when.' I don't have a doubt that the owner will want him back. We can't put time and effort into training him when we aren't going to get any return on the investment—"

"But they might not find his owner. Maybe his owner won't want him!"

Ian was gently shaking his head. "That isn't likely. Someone invested quite a bit of money in the colt. What surprises me is that the owner hasn't been tracked down or come forward yet." He paused. "Cindy, I'm not trying to be cruel, but I'm afraid you'll be hurt even more in the end if you get your hopes up now. Maybe it would be best to ask the Jockey Club to find somewhere else to board Glory until his owner is found."

"No!" Cindy cried. "He likes it here. He's learning to trust people again. He's happy! Someone else might not take as good care of him!" She had to blink her eyes to stop tears from forming.

Ian rose and came over to put his arm around her shoulders. "I know the kind of bond you can form with a special horse. I've certainly had strong feelings about some of the horses I've trained. The fact remains that Glory is going to have to leave here. There is nothing any of us can do about it. It's better not to get too close to him and be even more devastated when he goes. Isn't there another Whitebrook horse that you could spend time on? What about Mr. Wonderful or Precocious?"

"They already get tons of attention from Sammy and Ashleigh," Cindy choked out.

"What about those two orphans you slept with the first night you were here? You were the one who named them."

Cindy had frequently gone to visit Four Leaf Clover and Rainbow, who were now strapping weanlings, but the two orphans had formed a special bond with Len, who had nursed and cared for them. Len and Vic doted on them. Neither of the orphans needed a special savior the way Glory did, and Glory only had her. Cindy didn't tell her foster father what she was thinking. She understood that he was trying to keep her from being hurt, yet she couldn't push away her dreams for Glory. She couldn't stop caring about the colt.

"I'm sorry, Cindy," he added. "I wish the situation were different too . . . but it's not."

Cindy nodded with lowered eyes. She didn't want to show either of her foster parents the depth of her disappointment.

"Why don't we do something special this weekend?" Beth said. "Sammy told me that Tor's having a small show at the stable on Sunday. We could all go, and you could invite Heather."

Cindy knew about the show. Samantha had already asked her to go. "Yes, I'd like that," she said. "Heather would too."

"Good. We'll make a day's outing of it, and what about Mandy? Would she like to go?"

"She'd love it."

"Why don't you call her, then? We'll pick her up. The show starts at ten, doesn't it? We can pick her up about nine thirty." Beth paused, then added softly, "I know life doesn't seem fair sometimes—but I don't have to tell you that. Neither Ian nor I want to hurt you."

"I know," Cindy said. "I'll go call Mandy and Heather."

She went upstairs and used the phone in Samantha's room. Mandy was out with her father, but Mrs. Jarvis said that she was sure Mandy would love to go and that she'd make sure Mandy was ready on Sunday.

Next Cindy dialed Heather's number. She told her friend the details of her conversation with her foster father. "He's positive they'll find Glory's owner soon, and the owner will take Glory away. I want to cry just thinking about it!"

"I know how you feel, Cin, but he's not gone yet, and if your foster father won't train him, then we can keep training him ourselves."

"We don't know enough."

"Maybe Sammy would help," Heather suggested.

"I don't want to get her in trouble, and it would be kind of like going behind my foster father's back."

"I just thought of something," Heather said with sudden inspiration. "There are tons of training books in the stable office. Why don't you ask if you can borrow some? No one would mind, would they?"

"No—and if anyone asked why I wanted them, I could say I want to learn more about training, which is true." Cindy hesitated. "But I hate to do anything sneaky. I don't want to make Ian and Beth angry with me."

"Why would they get angry? No one's told you that you couldn't ride Glory."

"No."

"So you're not being sneaky. It's not like you're doing anything to hurt Glory, and you're not going to ride him on the training oval or anything."

"Right," Cindy said, feeling slightly more cheerful. "After school tomorrow, I'll ask if I can borrow some of the books." Yet as she hung up the phone and went into her room to change for bed, she knew nothing had changed. She would still lose Glory.

4

CINDY SELECTED SOME TRAINING BOOKS FROM THE OFFICE shelves the next afternoon, asking Mike, who was the only one around, if it was okay.

"Sure," he told her, then grinned. "It didn't take you long to get racing in your blood. Catching, isn't it?"

Cindy smiled, but wondered what Mike would say if he knew her real reason for borrowing the books. She brought them to her room and started poring through them that night after she'd finished her homework. There was so much to learn. Some of the training techniques were obvious, such as gradually increasing the length of workouts, but other technical details, like when to use blinders or a nose roll, were beyond her experience. She decided that for the time being, she and Heather would just have to stick to the basics.

They didn't have an opportunity to try even the basics over the next two days, since it rained steadily. It was much too wet to go riding. She and Heather had to content themselves with talking over their plans at school.

The weather cleared by Saturday night, and Sunday dawned clear and sunny. It would have been a perfect day to take Glory out, but they were going to the horse show, and Cindy knew she couldn't back out.

They left the farm at nine, first picking up Heather, who was excited about seeing her first real show, then stopping at the Jarvis house in suburban Lexington before going to Tor's stable on the outskirts of town.

The parking lot was already crowded with cars, pickups, and horse trailers. Although many of the entrants were regular boarders at the stable, others had come from private stables. Samantha had gone over early to help Tor and his father set up. Her friend, Yvonne Ortez, was helping out too, although Yvonne would also be competing on her Thoroughbred gelding, Cisco.

Since the weather had cleared, most classes would be held outdoors, with the balance in the large indoor ring.

"Can we go see Butterball first?" Mandy asked as they threaded through the crowd in the stable yard. Blanketed and tacked horses were being walked. Competitors, dressed in immaculate riding habits, tended their mounts, gathered tack, and stood in groups, talking. The stands set up outside the ring were filling, but Cindy knew Tor and Samantha would have already reserved seats for them.

"Of course we can visit Butterball," Beth said to

Mandy. "I was going to suggest it myself. I hear from Sammy that you two are doing really well."

Mandy grinned proudly. "We sure are. We're going to ride in the Pony Commando Christmas show." The Pony Commandos, all physically handicapped children about Mandy's age, met once a week at the stable for lessons and with Samantha and Tor's help were making great progress.

The large stable building was a hive of activity, too. In the stalls and in the aisles riders were giving their mounts a final grooming, braiding manes and tails, applying hoof oil. Human voices blended with the snorts and nickers of horses, but it wasn't chaotic. Although there was the occasional nervous titter, everyone seemed to know what they were doing. Cindy loved the atmosphere.

Butterball was stabled at one end of the barn with some of the other stable-owned ponies. The Jarvises had bought Butterball for Mandy for her birthday the previous spring, and the little girl doted on the pony. He fit his name. He was chubby and golden colored, but unlike many ponies, he had a sweet and willing disposition.

Cindy unlatched the stall door, and Mandy hobbled in to greet the pony. Her legs were gradually growing stronger, but the improvement was slow and often frustrating for the little girl.

"I brought you some carrots, Butterball," Mandy crooned. "We've come to watch the show, but I'll stop by later." The girl frowned and cast an appraising eye over the pony. "Looks like you've been out rolling in the dirt. I'll have to give you a good brushing, too."

The pony eyed her affectionately and continued munching. Mandy turned to Heather and beamed a smile. "Isn't he cute?"

"He sure is," Heather agreed. "I'll bet the two of you will get a ribbon at your Christmas show."

"We're getting better all the time. We've been practicing on some jumps . . . only crossbars," Mandy added.

"That's a good start," Beth said. "You have to begin with the basics."

"I know, but someday I want to be able to do big jumps like Tor and Yvonne."

Beth smiled. "I don't doubt for a minute that you will, but for now, I think we'd better find our seats or we'll miss the first classes."

They said good-bye to Butterball and moved back down the crowded aisle toward the exit.

Someone called out to them, "Hey, you guys. Aren't you even going to say hello?"

They turned to see Yvonne coming out of one of the stalls. Her straight shoulder-length black hair shone, and her dark eyes danced with mischief.

"We didn't even see you," Cindy said. "There's so much going on."

"Yeah. Great, isn't it?" Yvonne said. "I was just checking on Cisco."

"How is he?" Cindy asked.

"See for yourself." Yvonne motioned into the stall.

Cisco had come to the half-door to see what all the commotion was about. Although he was smaller, and his coat pure gray, not dappled, he reminded Cindy of Glory, and she felt an unexpected twinge of envy that Yvonne owned her special horse and didn't have to worry about losing him.

"Are you getting nervous?" Heather asked.

"Not yet," Yvonne said with a smile, "but our class doesn't go off until late afternoon. I'll be nervous enough by then." Yvonne was one of Tor's most promising students. She and Cisco had won quite a few ribbons.

"After competing in the National Horse Show, you still get nervous?" Heather asked.

"I don't know too many riders who don't get nervous. Even Tor still does, and look at the ribbons he and Top Hat have won."

Someone called to her from down the aisle. "Coming!" Yvonne called back. "See you guys later. Have fun!" She hurried off, and the others made their way out into the sunshine.

"I haven't seen Sammy yet," Cindy said, peering around at the crowd.

"I'm sure she's got her hands full helping Tor get ready," Beth replied. "I didn't realize there would be this many competitors."

"Neither did I," Cindy said. "I wonder where our seats are." As she spoke Tor waved to them from the judges' stand set up just outside the ring. He pointed up to the top of the bleachers where a section of seating had

46

been taped off. Beth waved her acknowledgment and they started up, Cindy and Heather helping Mandy manage the steps.

Cindy felt a growing bubble of excitement as she took in all the activity and studied the fit and athletic horses and riders. Four judges arrived at the viewing stand, and Tor showed them to their seats. Cindy finally saw Sammy standing near the gate to the ring. She had clipboard in hand and was giving instructions and information to various riders. She definitely had her hands full.

Ten minutes later Tor went to the microphone and welcomed everyone to the show. He introduced the judges and ran through the order of classes. "I hope both the competitors and spectators will have a worthwhile and enjoyable time today," he concluded. There was a loud round of applause, then Tor announced the first of the pony classes, Beginning Riders at Walk, Trot, and Canter.

Mandy watched raptly throughout the pony classes, and especially the jumping class. "Butterball and I are going to do that," she murmured to Cindy in a determined voice.

"I know you are," Cindy told her. And she prayed the gutsy girl would overcome her obstacles.

The junior divisions came next, and both Cindy and Heather watched with concentration as riders close to their own age guided their mounts over the moderately difficult jump course. To Cindy, who had never jumped, the course seemed more than moderately difficult, and it took its toll on several riders who knocked down rails and had run-outs. She sympathized when she saw their disappointed faces as they rode out of the ring.

"I'm going to get some drinks," Beth said quietly. "Do you all want one?"

They all nodded, absorbed in what was going on in the ring. By the time Beth returned with four cans of lemonade, the junior division had finished and ribbons had been awarded.

"It must be so exciting to ride in to collect a ribbon," Heather said with a touch of awe in her voice.

"I know," Cindy agreed. The feeling had to be a lot like standing in the winner's circle after winning a race. A crew had entered the ring and were dismantling, rearranging, and rebuilding jumps. "They're setting up the more advanced course. Whew! Look at the size of some of them."

Heather nodded. "Is this the course Yvonne's going to jump?"

"I guess." Cindy looked down at her program. "But her class doesn't go off for a couple of hours."

"The intermediate classes go first," Mandy explained. "Then there's a half-hour break before the advanced classes. The fences will be even higher. Tor told us about it at our last Pony Commando lesson."

Cindy and Heather stared at her. "Higher?"

Mandy gave them a smile. "Yup. But Yvonne and Cisco can do it."

"What about the other riders?" Cindy asked.

"Some of them are from other stables, so I don't know about them. The best rider here besides Yvonne is

48

Angelique Dubret." Mandy wrinkled her nose. "She's stuck up, but she's good, and so is her horse, Appraiser."

Cindy remembered seeing Angelique and her horse at the stable. She had also thought Angelique was a snob and had sensed that Samantha and Angelique didn't get along.

"Is anyone hungry but me?" Beth asked. "Maybe this would be a good time to have our lunch—before Yvonne rides."

They all agreed. Despite her excitement, Cindy's stomach was rumbling. They helped Mandy down the risers, and after Beth collected the picnic basket from the car, they found a sunny spot under the now nearly bare-branched trees and spread out a blanket. Although there was a nip in the November air, the sun was warm and bright, and they weren't uncomfortable.

There was plenty to see as they ate. The ponies had all been brought back to the barn or their trailers, but some of the horses who'd recently competed were being walked, and the riders in the advanced classes were now milling around, leading their horses or riding them out to the warm-up area.

Cindy saw Yvonne leading Cisco from the barn. She had braided the gelding's mane and part of his tail, and his coat was shining and spotless. She stopped to talk to another rider, then mounted and rode out to the warm-up area herself.

"Let's go watch," Cindy said.

"You girls go ahead," Beth told them. "I'll clean up the picnic stuff and meet you back at the ring."

They headed toward the warm-up area behind the stable buildings. Several riders were trotting or cantering in circles, or taking their mounts over the warm-up jumps. Yvonne saw the girls and smiled, although Cindy could see the nervous tension on her face. Yvonne was circling Cisco at an easy posting trot when another rider approached. Cindy recognized Angelique and her big warmblood. Angelique's habit was immaculate, and her blond hair was gathered in a netted chignon at the back of her neck. She sat easily and confidently in the saddle, and there didn't seem to be a trace of nervousness on her pretty features.

"She thinks she's going to win," Mandy said, following Cindy's gaze.

"Could she beat Yvonne?"

"Maybe. She's ridden in tons of shows, but I don't think she knows how hard Yvonne has been practicing."

"I'll be rooting for Yvonne," Heather said loyally.

"Everyone is. Nobody likes Angelique very much. But she is good."

The grandstand was overflowing by the time Yvonne's advanced class began. Cindy studied the new course with a frown. The jumps were varied, and she wasn't even sure what a lot of them were called, but she knew that Yvonne and Cisco would have to be together every inch of the way if they hoped to go clean.

The riders entered the ring to walk the course—the first and only chance they would have to judge the fences before they competed. The earliest riders would have it the hardest. Later riders would be able judge the difficulties of the course from the mistakes and faults the early riders made.

Cindy was dismayed to see that of the twelve competitors, Yvonne was riding fourth, Angelique last. She silently wished Yvonne good luck.

The riders left the course, several of them looking grim. A few minutes later the first competitor rode into the ring, saluted the judges, put her horse into a canter, and circled to the first fence. They jumped clean through the first six fences, then she badly misjudged the distance to the next obstacle—a switchback to a two-fence combination. They took down the rail on the second fence. Both horse and rider were obviously rattled, and they fell apart, taking down rails at two more fences before finishing the course in well over optimum time. The rider looked close to tears as she left the ring. Tor announced the next competitor, a young man on a leggy chestnut.

He managed to go clean through the combination, but went too wide on the turn to the next fence. His mount's rear hooves caught the rail and knocked it down. The rider seemed to pull himself together, though, and took the next two fences flawlessly, but in order to make up time he rushed through the final three-fence combination and knocked down another rail.

"Whew, this is tough!" murmured Heather. "I'm glad I'm not Yvonne. No wonder she gets nervous."

Cindy glanced over to the gate, where Yvonne and the remaining competitors were waiting. Yvonne was mounted, walking Cisco in a small circle to keep him limber. She and the others watched the ring as the next competitor went out.

That rider did even worse. Her mount continually tried to run headlong between the fences. The rider couldn't keep him collected, and they came up much too close to the fifth fence, a wall. The horse slid to a stop and refused to jump. After two more refusals, they were disqualified.

It was Yvonne's turn. Cindy crossed the fingers on both hands as she watched Yvonne and Cisco enter the ring. Yvonne nodded to the judges, then put Cisco into a canter. It was impossible to tell Yvonne's state of mind, but Cindy could see that Yvonne was totally concentrated on the course ahead. She and Cisco cleared the first four fences smoothly, but that was the easy part. The second half of the course was what had caused the earlier riders problems.

They cleared the wall with a strong leap. Cisco really seemed to be putting his heart into it. Immediately Yvonne began turning him into the switchback toward the two-fence combination, cutting the corner tight to save valuable seconds against the clock. Their approach to the combination was perfect, and they sailed over. "The best so far," Cindy whispered hoarsely to Heather and Mandy, but she knew it was much too soon to relax. Six fences to go. Yvonne was riding aggressively, yet cautiously, taking nothing for granted. Cindy felt as if her heart was going over each of the fences with them as Yvonne and Cisco cleared a parallel, a hedge and a ditch, a gate. Finally they were turning toward the last obstacle, the three-fence combination.

"Don't lose it now!" Mandy whispered urgently.

Yvonne and Cisco moved toward the combination at an even, collected canter. Cisco gathered and soared over the first fence, landed, gathered and lifted, landed, gathered and lifted.

His rear hooves ticked the top rail. Cindy gasped. The rail shivered for an instant—but stayed in place. Yvonne and Cisco had finished with a clean round!

The girls hugged each other. Yvonne's smile was brilliant as she circled Cisco and patted his neck to loud applause.

"Wow! She did it," Mandy cried. "I knew they could!"

Cindy was thrilled for Yvonne, but there were eight more competitors still to ride, including Angelique. If any of them jumped clean, with as good a time as Yvonne, there would be a jump-off.

One after another they tried and came up short. Then Angelique rode out. Cindy sat tensely. Angelique definitely looked confident, and she rode with grace. Her big warmblood sailed over the fences, seeming to do it effortlessly. They'd ridden three-quarters of the course clean. An anxious knot was forming in Cindy's stomach. But Angelique was riding against the clock now. She not only had to go clean, but she had to beat Yvonne's time. Angelique was still clean coming up to the last combination, yet even to Cindy's unschooled eye, she seemed to be rushing, cutting corners a little too tight.

Again Cindy held her breath as Angelique and Appraiser sailed over the first two fences in the combination.

Heather groaned. "They're going to beat Yvonne. Their time is better."

But Angelique, in her race against the clock, had miscalculated. Her mount was too flattened out over the last fence. His rear hooves rapped the top rail—and this time, it did come down. Yvonne had won it!

Angelique's face was tight with anger when she rode off the course, but the girls were elated and cheered Yvonne at the top of their lungs when she and Cisco rode into the ring to collect the blue ribbon.

"So," Beth said happily, "I guess we all enjoyed ourselves today."

"Yes!" they answered in one voice.

5

WHEN CINDY AND HEATHER MET FOR LUNCH THE NEXT DAY IN school, they talked about the show. "I loved watching the jumping," Heather said. "I'd love to learn to jump myself."

"You could take lessons at Tor's," Cindy told her.

Heather wagged her head. "My parents can't afford lessons. I asked for lessons before I met you, but my father had lost his job. They didn't have any extra money."

"He's got another job now, doesn't he?"

"Yeah, but not as good as the one he lost."

Cindy took a sip of milk, then looked over to Heather. "I've got an idea! Sammy and Tor always need help with the Pony Commandos. Why don't you volunteer? I'll bet Tor would give you some free lessons in return."

"Do you think so?" Heather asked eagerly. "But he's so busy already, and I'd be embarrassed to ask."

"What about Yvonne? If Tor would let you borrow one of the stable horses, Yvonne could teach you."

Heather looked doubtful. "I don't know Yvonne that well either."

"The Pony Commandos have a lesson on Wednesday. I already told Sammy I'd help. It's easy—you just help the kids get in and out of the saddle and lead them around the ring if they need it. Sammy's going to pick me up at school. Come with me, and if you feel funny about asking for help from Tor or Yvonne, I'll ask them."

"No!" Heather cried. "Then I'd really be embarrassed."

Cindy smiled. "I wouldn't tell them that you knew I was asking. I'd just say that you'd really like to learn to jump, but your parents can't afford lessons. I'll bet they'll offer to give you some free help."

"Haven't you ever wanted to try jumping?"

"I've thought about it," Cindy said more seriously, "especially after seeing the show yesterday. But Glory's more important right now. If I have any extra time, I want to spend it training him. I want the others to see how good he is before it's too late. You're still coming home with me this afternoon to help?"

"You bet. I can't wait!"

The girls were chattering happily when they got off the bus at the end of the Whitebrook drive and hurried into the cottage to change.

After donning jeans, boots, heavy sweatshirts, and hard hats, they crossed the yard and followed the lane to a nearby paddock. Since the day was sunny and close to fifty degrees, Len and Vic had put the horses out for the day.

Glory was in a paddock with several actively racing geldings and Bo Jangles. Cindy went to the fence and whistled. Glory immediately lifted his head, then trotted to the paddock fence, anticipating the treat that Cindy always brought him. He happily gobbled up the carrot she gave him. Cindy opened the paddock gate and clipped his lead shank to his halter. "We're going for a ride, big guy," she said. "I'll bet you'll be glad to get out on the lanes after all the rain we had last week."

Glory snorted his eagerness and willingly followed Cindy out of the paddock. Heather collected Bo Jangles, who had come for his treat too, then carefully latched the gate behind them.

"First, we'll give you a good brushing," Cindy told the big colt, rubbing his nose as she led him toward the barn. "Then we've got some new stuff to try."

She led Glory inside, pausing so both of them could adjust their eyes to the dimmer light. Heather and Bo Jangles followed. Most of the stall doors were open, and Vic was farther down the aisle, forking out fresh bedding. He looked up and smiled when he saw them, then a frown creased his brow.

Before Cindy had a chance to ask him if something was wrong, her foster father stepped out of his office and walked toward the girls. His face was set, as if he'd just heard bad news.

"We heard from the Jockey Club today," he said quickly. "They've traced Glory's owner."

Cindy's heart plummeted to her feet.

"I know this isn't good news for you," he added gently, "but we knew the day would come. Glory's description and blood type match those of a colt registered by a small breeding farm in Virginia. His altered tattoo is close enough to the original tattoo that there can't be any question Glory is that horse."

"But—but why didn't they report him stolen?" Cindy rushed out. Her throat felt so tight, she could barely swallow.

"Because they didn't realize the colt was gone until the Jockey Club notified them. It's all pretty complicated, and the Jockey Club and the police are still looking into it. The farm was owned by a young man who had only been in the business for a few years. Sadly, he was killed in a car accident about the same time Glory must have been stolen. He wasn't married and lived at the farm alone. He only had one full-time employee, a combination manager-groom. The employee disappeared right after the owner's death. The police are trying to track him down, because it seems obvious he was involved in the horse-switching operation.

"The lawyers for the young man's estate have hired temporary help to look after the remaining stock—about eight mares and weanlings and a couple of two-year-olds. When the Jockey Club notified them, they went through all the farm records and could find no trace of Glory's papers, except the duplicates filed with the Jockey Club. Glory was foaled by one of the farm's mares, who was bred to an outside stallion. The owner obviously seems to have wanted to race the colt, since Glory was sent to a training center as a two-year-old. He'll turn three this January, by the way."

"If his owner is dead," Cindy asked hoarsely, "then who owns him now? I don't understand."

"He's the property of the young man's estate."

Cindy was wagging her head, partly out of shock, partly out of confusion.

"The way the law works," Ian explained gently, "is that when someone dies, their estate—all the property and assets they own after debts are paid—goes into probate until it's distributed to the heirs. There are taxes to be paid, of course, but I won't go into that. The young man had only one surviving relative—a sister—and he willed everything to her."

"So she's going to take over the farm? She's Glory's new owner?"

"She will be when all the legalities are sorted out, but she's not going to take over the farm. She lives in California and doesn't know anything about her brother's business—or have any interest in it. The lawyers handling the estate called here today. The farm and all the stock are to be sold at auction to settle the estate and pay all the inheritance taxes. The stock will be sold at the January Keeneland auction, since the attorneys feel that's where they'll bring the best price."

Cindy tried to digest it all. Glory fidgeted, not understanding the delay in his grooming. Cindy absently rubbed his neck. "If everything's going to be sold," she said finally, "then we could buy Glory!"

Cindy felt a momentary spurt of hope, but then remembered her situation. She had no money; the McLeans had already been so good to her, but she knew they didn't have a lot of extra money. She'd seen how careful Beth was with household expenses.

"I wish it were that easy, Cindy," her foster father sympathized. "He's had some training, but he's unproven. Even considering the question of his potential, we couldn't afford the price they'll ask. He's decently, if not spectacularly, bred. His dam, though she never raced, comes from a line of proven stamina. His sire is Great Beyond, who had an excellent record during his racing career, but has been inconsistent at stud. He's sired a few very good horses, but he has a fairly high percentage of nonwinners. With that combination of bloodlines, Glory would be worth the risk to some buyers, but the risk would be high. The odds are less than fifty-fifty that he inherited his sire's talent."

"He does have talent—" Cindy began, then stopped. Yes, she believed that Glory had talent just waiting to be tapped, but she also knew she was far too inexperienced to know what qualities made a good racehorse.

"I'm sorry, Cindy. I know how much the colt means to you. There's one strange coincidence, though. The colt's registered name is March to Glory."

Cindy and Heather both stared at Ian. "He really is Glory?" Cindy said with a gasp. "Heather and I only decided to call him that because he was so beautiful and so proud."

"I know. I was pretty amazed myself."

"It's almost like I was meant to have him," Cindy said under her breath, then looked up at her foster father. "Couldn't you just try him on the track . . . before he's sent to the auction?" she pleaded. "If he does have talent, maybe Mike and Ashleigh would buy him!"

Her foster father shook his head. "I can't, Cindy. I don't have the owner or her attorney's permission. They've agreed to let Glory stay here until the auction—in fact, they asked if we'd consider boarding him, since we're right in Lexington. They're paying us, of course, and expect the colt to stay in top condition. It would be unethical for me to put him in training without their okay."

"But couldn't you ask them?"

"I doubt very much they'd agree. The settling of the estate is purely a business transaction for them. They're not going to pay the additional expense of training fees. Besides, Glory has been out of training for months. You can't take an unconditioned horse out onto the track and ask him to work. That would be dangerously stressful. It could cause injury, and it would take weeks to condition him by gradually building up stamina and muscle. It's like training a human athlete. You can't expect someone who's only jogged around the block a few times to go out and train with the Olympic team."

Ian laid his hand on Cindy's shoulder. "I'm afraid you're just going to have to accept the fact that Glory isn't ours—that someone else will make the decisions about his future. I know how you feel," he sympathized, "but there'll be other horses you can work with, sweetheart, and I'm sure Glory will go to a good home."

All Cindy could think of was the abuse he'd already received at the neighbors'. Not all owners and trainers were as good to their horses as the people at Whitebrook. She swallowed back her tears. "Can I still ride him, though . . . until they take him away?"

"I don't see why not," Ian said gently, his eyes sad. "The exercise will be good for him, and I know you'll be careful. Were you girls planning to ride today?"

Cindy nodded.

"Have fun, then, and I'm sorry I had to bring you bad news."

After he returned to his office, Cindy and Heather exchanged stricken looks. "Oh, Cin," Heather said. "What are you going to do?"

Cindy shook her head. "I don't know. I can't think straight. Everybody warned me that he couldn't stay here forever, but I can't stand the thought of him going—of someone else having him. What if they don't love him like I do? What if they mistreat him?"

"We've got to figure out some way that you can keep him. How much do you think he's worth?"

"I don't know. I could ask Sammy."

"I have some money saved from baby-sitting," Heather offered.

"He'd cost a lot more than that." Suddenly Glory nudged her with his nose. "I'm sorry, boy," Cindy said, realizing that they were still standing motionless. "You don't understand what's going on, do you? Let's get you brushed. At least I can still ride you."

They put the horses in crossties and carefully

brushed them before collecting their tack. The girls were both silent, lost in misery and thought. They only spoke again when they were out on the lane, heading away from the stable yard.

"I could take Glory and run away," Cindy said.

Heather looked over sharply. "No, Cindy. Don't even think about it! Anyway, how would that make things better? Where could you go? How would you take care of yourself? I thought you loved Whitebrook! You told me this is the first time you've ever felt like you had a home."

Cindy flushed and felt ashamed of herself. She didn't know why she'd even thought of running away. "I'm just desperate, I guess," she murmured. "I can't think of any other way to keep Glory. I do love it here. I don't want to leave, and I want Ian and Beth to adopt me. I just wish Glory could stay, too."

"You still have over a month before Glory goes to auction. When is the Keeneland auction?"

"The first week in January. I heard Ashleigh and Mike talking about it the other day. They're planning to go."

"There's time, then. Things could change. We can keep trying to train Glory."

Cindy was thinking about what her foster father had said and was realizing that the plans she and Heather had for training Glory were pretty far-fetched. "We don't know enough, Heather," she said, suddenly feeling very unsure of herself and her abilities. "How do we get him in condition?"

"Those training books you borrowed must have said something about that."

"I only skimmed that part. I didn't even think about conditioning. He looks so healthy. I didn't think there was more to it than that." Cindy paused, then frowned thoughtfully. "I do remember reading something about long canters and slow gallops—I mean long—like a couple of miles."

Heather brightened. "Well, we could do that. There are miles of lanes here."

Cindy was beginning to catch some of Heather's optimism. "Right. We could start with long canters, and if Glory seemed to be getting tired, we could slow down to a trot. But what about Bo?"

"He may not be able to move as fast, but he's probably in better condition than Glory. Don't your foster dad and Mike use him in workouts all the time to pace the other horses?"

"They do!" Cindy's brain was suddenly churning with ideas. "How about if we start today by cantering for a mile—though I'm not exactly sure how far a mile is over the lanes. If he gets tired, we'll slow down to a trot. But we'll do the same the next day, and every day, until he's not tired at the end of a mile. Then we increase the distance—we'll have to look through the training books when we go back to the cottage and see what they say about distance. Anyway, when he canters, say, two miles without getting tired, then we do slow gallops for a short distance. . . ." Cindy stopped and looked over to Heather. "I haven't galloped before. I'm not sure how. I know I have to keep him in control—that's what Sammy and Ashleigh do with the horses they breeze—or he'll run away with me, but I don't know if I'm good enough."

"Don't worry about that now. It sounds like it will be a while before you can gallop him. But you know that you can ride him at a canter. Let's do it!"

"The only thing," Cindy said, feeling a prick of conscience, "is that I don't have anyone's permission to gallop Glory. I know my foster father thinks we only walk and trot the horses out here. Sammy does too, or they wouldn't let me take Glory out. I don't have enough experience."

"Grown-ups aren't always right," Heather said with a touch of unexpected defiance. "They're always telling you they're doing things for your own good—like my parents saying that in a couple of years I'll outgrow my love of horses—like your foster father saying that you'll find another horse to love as much as Glory. How do they know that? I don't think I'll stop loving horses and riding in a few years. You're not going to stop loving Glory. I think that sometimes grown-ups are dead wrong. I think this is one of those times we have to prove them wrong."

Cindy looked over to her friend with admiration in her eyes. She supposed she had questioned grown-up decisions all her life by running away from the miserable foster homes they'd chosen for her. She smiled. "So do I. We won't know unless we try. Right?"

"Right!"

6

CINDY AND HEATHER CANTERED THE HORSES FOR WHAT THEY estimated to be a mile that afternoon, then trotted them back to the stables, groomed them, and returned them to their stalls. Then they went up to Cindy's bedroom to do their homework and study the training books until Heather's mother came to pick her up at five thirty.

Only Beth and Cindy were home for dinner. Ian had gone to a meeting with some other horsemen in town, and Samantha had a late class.

"I was sorry to hear about Glory," Beth said as they sat down. "I know how much you'll miss him. Do you want to talk about it? Sometimes that helps."

Cindy shook her head. "Thanks, but it makes me too sad."

"I understand. At least you'll have his company for another month or so. I know that's not much consolation, but a lot could happen in a month."

Cindy looked up, wondering what Beth meant. But from Beth's expression, Cindy could tell that her foster mother was just trying to cheer her up.

They talked about school and the Pony Commandos over dinner, which Cindy had to force herself to eat. She couldn't wait for Samantha to get home so she could ask the older girl what she thought Glory was worth. If it wasn't too, too much, maybe she and Heather could raise the money to buy him. While she did the dishes, Cindy tried to think of ways to make some extra money, but she didn't come up with any brilliant ideas. All she had was her weekly allowance, and there weren't many baby-sitting jobs so far out from Lexington.

Instead of going into the living room to watch TV, she went to take a shower, then curled up on her bed with the training books. She must have dozed, because she suddenly jerked up with a start when her book slid off the bed and crashed on the floor. Glancing at her clock, she saw that she'd been asleep for over an hour. Was Samantha home yet? she wondered. Cindy threw her legs over the side of the bed and went out into the small upstairs hall. She heard Ian and Beth talking downstairs. Samantha's bedroom door was half-open and her light was on. Cindy went over and knocked.

"Sammy, can I come in?" she asked.

"Sure," Samantha called. Samantha was sprawled on her bed with a notebook spread open in front of her and a pen in her hand. Samantha's long red hair was pulled back with combs to keep it off her face.

"You're doing your homework," Cindy said.

Samantha smiled. "That's okay. I'm making notes, and I'm getting bored. I don't mind an interruption." She patted the edge of her bed. "Sit down."

Cindy did.

Before Cindy could speak, though, Samantha said, "Dad and Beth told me when I got home that they've found Glory's owner. I'm sorry, Cin. I know how much you'll miss him."

Cindy had already begun thinking of Samantha as her real sister. Even though Samantha was six years older, she didn't treat Cindy like a stupid little kid. She was interested in what Cindy thought and felt, and so often sympathized. Cindy didn't feel any hesitation in talking to her. "I was hoping they'd never find his owner," Cindy said. "You've seen the difference in him since he's been here. You remember how spooky and scared he was at first. He's not like that now."

"I know," Samantha said sadly. "He's learning how to trust again, thanks to all the love and care you've given him. The change in his attitude reminds me a lot of the change in Shining after she got care and love."

"I can't stand to think of him going to some strange place with people he doesn't know."

Samantha reached over and took Cindy's hand. "I know exactly how you feel, sweetie. It's the same way I felt right after we moved here from Townsend Acres, and Clay Townsend wanted to sell his half-interest in Pride to a stranger. I wish there was something I could do to help."

"Do you know how much Glory is worth—how much someone would pay for him at the auction?"

Samantha looked like she didn't really want to answer the question. "I can't be sure, Cindy. With his bloodlines and his conformation, maybe ten thousand dollars . . . maybe less, maybe more. It depends on what kind of buyers come to the auction, what they're looking for and how much they want to spend. Prices have gone down in the last few years, but the Japanese have become big buyers and have been willing to pay the price for good racing and breeding stock. Racing is very popular in Japan."

"The Japanese?" Cindy was dumbfounded. Japan was on the other side of the world! Glory could be sold to someone in Japan?

"I'm not saying the Japanese will buy him," Samantha said quickly. "Only that they can drive up auction prices. So can the Arab and European interests."

"And that means Glory could be sold for even more," Cindy responded dismally.

"No one knows what's going to happen at an auction. I've been to a couple with my father and Ashleigh and Mike. Sometimes there aren't any big buyers there at all, and the bidding doesn't meet the reserve—that means no one bids up to the minimum price the sellers have set. Other times the prices go higher than expected."

Cindy's heart had already sunk to her feet when Samantha had mentioned ten thousand dollars. She had been thinking in hundreds, not thousands. To her it seemed a phenomenal amount of money. The most she'd ever had in her pocket was five dollars. It was more money than she had ever thought about having, and more extra money than she thought her foster parents had to spend.

"There's always the chance the horse won't meet the reserve," Samantha added, "and the owners will sell privately for less."

"Ten thousand dollars," Cindy repeated. It was so much money. How could she could ask her foster parents, or even Mike and Ashleigh, to spend that much money on Glory? "Do you really think someone might pay that much for him?" she asked bleakly.

Samantha squeezed Cindy's hand. "I can't tell you that for sure, Cindy. He's the kind of horse someone might take a chance on."

"But not Whitebrook."

"Not right now," Samantha answered gently. "They couldn't afford to take that kind of a risk."

They talked a while longer before Cindy went to bed. Cindy knew Samantha hurt for her and understood exactly how she felt, but what could Samantha do?

She and Heather had no choice, Cindy decided as she pulled up her covers and turned off her light. They would have to train Glory themselves and, before he was sent to auction, prove to everyone at Whitebrook that he had talent and was worth keeping on the farm.

Cindy was glad that the long Thanksgiving weekend was coming up. She found it almost impossible to concentrate in school the next day. All she could think about was Glory. She was filled with relief when the final bell rang and she met Heather in the hallway. Samantha would be waiting out front to drive them to Tor's stable for the Pony Commando lesson.

Heather hadn't taken the news of Glory's value any better than Cindy had. "I've been thinking all day," she said. "Never in a million years could we make ten thousand dollars! I didn't know horses were worth that much."

"Sammy said that good racehorses can sell for a lot more than that. Ten thousand dollars is a low price."

Heather groaned. "We'll think of something, Cindy."

"We'll just have to keep training him," Cindy said with determination. "Maybe it won't do any good, but at least we'll have tried. We won't have much time, though. It's getting colder and the ground could freeze. And it gets dark so early."

"We'll do it."

Samantha honked when she saw them, and they hurried to her car. "Feeling any better?" she asked Cindy.

"No. It would be hard to feel any better."

"I know," Samantha said softly. "At least maybe the Commando lesson will take your mind off it for a while. Thanks for offering to help, Heather. We need it. We lost some of our volunteers, and even though the kids are getting much better, we still need at least four helpers."

As soon as they arrived at the stable, they went inside to get the ponies ready for the arrival of the six Commandos. Tor hurried over to greet them. "Good,

71

you're here! Welcome to the Commandos, Heather. You couldn't have picked a better time to start. Yvonne just called. She needs to spend the afternoon in the university library doing research for a paper."

"Ah," Samantha said. "She was afraid her English Lit professor was going to give the class an extra project. We'll manage, Tor. Cindy, you and Heather can start by bringing out Zorro and Dandy and putting them in the last two crossties."

For the next half hour they worked steadily, bringing the ponies from their stalls, brushing them, collecting their saddles and bridles from the tack room, and tacking them up. When they finished with Zorro and Dandy, they brought out two more ponies. Samantha prepared Milk Dud and Mandy's pony, Butterball. They led the ponies to the indoor ring in twos just as the six students arrived.

Mandy hurried over with a smile. "Oh, Heather, you're helping out today? Super!" Mandy took Butterball's reins from Samantha and crooned to the pony. Janet Roarsh, who worked with the children in physical therapy and had started the riding program with Beth, Tor, and Samantha's help, pushed forward Timmy, one of the wheelchair-bound students. Samantha helped the other wheelchair-bound student, Robert. Cindy and Heather led the remaining ponies to their riders, Aaron, Charmaine, and Jane. The Commandos had been meeting for over a year, and the students' confidence and skills had improved amazingly in that time. Cindy knew from Janet and Beth how much the children looked forward to their hour at the stable. They were all smiling and eager as they were helped up onto their ponies' backs.

"What are we going to do today?" Charmaine asked excitedly.

"We're going to practice our trots and figure eights," Samantha said, "then work on cavalletti, and if everyone does well, we'll do some simple jumps." Although Samantha didn't have Tor or Yvonne's skills at jumping, she'd had some experience, particularly in helping train and ride Mike's steeplechaser, Sierra.

"All right!" several of them called, including Mandy, who was the best student in the class and desperately wanted to learn to jump.

The class had progressed beyond leading reins, and all Samantha, Cindy, and Heather had to do was walk alongside the mounted riders, ready in case anyone needed advice or help.

Cindy noticed how much Heather seemed to be enjoying the lesson, smiling and talking with the young riders. The class spent the first forty-five minutes reinforcing the basics, then Samantha told everyone to stop. She went to the side of the ring and set up three low jumps; first a low crossbar, or X, then two single-rail fences with the crosspiece set in the lowest position. She then explained to the class what she wanted them to do.

"Last lesson you all got a chance to jump over the X at a trot. Today we're going to jump the X, then continue on and jump the two single-rail fences. Those of you who can get into a hunt seat, do. Those who can't, just sit firm in the saddle. Stay in a trot over all three fences. Remember, keep your heads up and your eyes forward. I want to see straight backs and shoulders. Any questions? No? Then who wants to go first?"

Mandy instantly volunteered. "Keep to a trot," Samantha told her. "Don't let Butterball break stride between the fences."

The little girl nodded and set off at a trot, circling toward the first jump. Cindy watched a little nervously. Mandy still didn't have that much strength in her legs. But Mandy trotted confidently over all three jumps, grinning as she rode back to the others.

"Perfect!" Samantha praised. "Okay, next!"

One by one the students trotted their ponies over the jumps. A couple had problems keeping their ponies going, so Samantha walked alongside, encouraging them. Finally everyone had cleared the jumps successfully.

"Okay. Well done!" Samantha called. "That's it for today. We'll do some more jumping next week."

Cindy, Heather, Samantha, and Janet helped the children from their mounts. Those who would be riding home with Janet in the van waved good-bye. Mandy always stayed to groom Butterball, and her mother would pick her up later.

They led the ponies back into the stable area, untacked them, brushed them, and put them in their stalls, giving each of them a carrot for a reward. Except on the hottest days, the ponies never needed to be cooled out. They hadn't been worked hard enough to overheat and sweat.

While Heather was putting the last pony away, Cindy approached Samantha and spoke quietly. "Sammy, you know Heather really wants to learn to jump, but her family can't afford lessons. I was just wondering, since she's going to be volunteering here once a week, whether you think Tor might let her use one of the stable horses for a half hour or so and give her some pointers. I know it's a lot to ask. . . . "

Samantha was smiling. "I don't know why I didn't think of it myself. I think that's a great idea, and Tor will too. He's got a lesson now, but I'll talk to him later and see what we can arrange."

"Don't say anything to Heather about my asking," Cindy said quickly.

"Nope. We'll keep it a surprise."

"Thanks, Sammy! She's going to be thrilled."

Samantha ruffled Cindy's blond hair. "You're really a good kid. I hope we can work out something for you and Glory."

Cindy sure hoped so too, but at the moment she wasn't very optimistic. Just the same, she forced herself to think positively. She and Heather would somehow work a miracle.

7

THE NEXT MORNING CINDY AND SAMANTHA HELPED BETH prepare Thanksgiving dinner. Ashleigh, Mike, and Gene Reese were going to Ashleigh's parents for dinner, so Beth had invited Len and Vic, and Samantha had invited Tor. When the turkey was in the oven and all the vegetables prepared, Cindy excused herself and went out to visit Glory. As a Thanksgiving treat, she'd brought along a special ration of choice, tender baby carrots. The colt loved them.

Cindy settled down on the bedding in his stall as he chomped. The kitten, Imp, joined them. Cindy had brought some treats for the cats too, and Imp quickly jumped down from the stall partition to gobble them up from the palm of her hand. She stroked his soft fur, and he purred contentedly.

This was her first Thanksgiving in her new home. It had never been much of a holiday in her previous foster homes—no holidays had been that special. At Christmas, maybe she got one gift, and that never turned out to be anything she especially wanted—usually a practical gift like new socks and underwear or new pajamas, which her foster parents would have had to buy for her anyway. She'd never had any reason to believe in Santa Claus.

Cindy was looking forward to the happy gathering around the big table, which Beth and Samantha had moved to the living room of the cottage for the occasion. Her foster father had already brought in wood for the big stone fireplace.

Yet Cindy couldn't push away the heavy feeling inside her. If she couldn't find a way to keep Glory on the farm, what would she do without him? Of course there were other horses that she loved—Shining and Wonder and Pride, and Mr. Wonderful and Precocious. It was different, though, from what she felt for Glory. She'd rescued him, hidden him away and cared for him herself—even though she'd known that hiding him could get her into a lot of trouble and possibly jeopardize her chances of staying with the McLeans. Saving Glory had been worth all the risks, though, every one of them.

Glory lowered his head and breathed gently into her hair. Cindy lifted a hand to caress his muzzle. "And pretty soon you'll be gone," she murmured to the horse. "That's not much of a reason to celebrate Thanksgiving."

As soon as the words were out of her mouth, she felt ashamed of herself. How could she even think that she had nothing to be thankful for? Seven months ago she wouldn't have dreamed that someday she would be living on a wonderful farm like Whitebrook, with people who truly cared about her and wanted to adopt her—that she would have made such wonderful friends and learned to trust people again.

"I'm wrong, Glory. I have a lot to be thankful for, and even if you have to go, we'll at least have had a little bit of time together. I just wish it could be longer."

Glory huffed softly, his sweet breath tickling her ear. "You understand, don't you?" She smiled and pushed herself up from the bedding. She heard footsteps in the aisle outside the stall and turned.

Len was looking in at her and Glory. He was dressed in his only suit, his grizzled beard freshly trimmed. "Should have guessed you'd be here," he said with a teasing grin. "I was just heading up to your place. My mouth's watering already."

Cindy brushed off her jeans. "I should be going too, and see if Beth needs any more help." She kissed Glory on the nose and let herself out of the stall.

"I'm right sorry about Glory," Len said as they left the barn and crossed the yard. "I know how attached you are, and I can see the difference in the colt since you've been looking after him. Sometimes things just don't go the way you'd like, but don't be too discouraged. He's not gone yet."

Cindy managed a wobbly smile. "No, he's not gone yet."

———

When they opened the cottage door, they were greeted by the delicious smell of roasting turkey. A fire was crackling on the hearth in the living room. Vic and Ian were standing by the fire, talking. Tor had arrived and was helping Samantha set the table.

"Happy Thanksgiving," Len called cheerily.

"And the same to you, Len. Come on over by the fire and warm yourself," Ian said.

"I'd be glad to. There's a nip in the air today."

Cindy took off her jacket and hung it on the rack, then sprinted upstairs to change out of her jeans. She hadn't known what to expect, but she saw that everyone else had dressed up. Cindy pawed through her closet and chose a loose, long-waisted blue dress that Beth had bought for her that fall. She pulled a pair of tights out of the drawer and changed out of her jeans and shirt. After pulling on her tights, she drew the dress over her head, then searched in the closet for her flats and slipped her feet into them. She went to the dresser and quickly drew the brush through her shining blond hair, then hurried back downstairs.

The men were still talking by the fire. Cindy went into the kitchen and asked if she could help.

Beth was stirring creamed onions on the stove top. Samantha was basting the turkey. "The potatoes are done, if you don't mind mashing them," Beth said. "I've already added the butter and milk."

Cindy set to work with the mixer and put the pot back on the stove when she was finished. Beth, looking very relaxed for someone who'd just cooked a huge dinner, glanced around the kitchen and nodded to herself. "I think we're all set. If the turkey's done, Sammy, I'll get your father to come in and carve it. There's not enough room to carve at the table."

Len looked in through the kitchen doorway. "I'd be glad to do the carving," he offered. "It's not often that Vic and I cook ourselves up a meal like this. And I used to be pretty good at carving as a younger man when my whole family got together at my grandparents' place."

Beth smiled. "Sure, Len, if you'd like. Ian's going to be busy enough after dinner. Since this is a liberated household, the men have been assigned cleanup duty."

Len chuckled. "So if I carve the turkey, I won't be handed a dish towel?"

Beth's blue eyes twinkled. "I may let you off, but no promises."

Len took off his suit jacket and rolled up his sleeves, and took the turkey from the oven. As he carved, Cindy, Samantha, and Beth dished the rest of the food into serving bowls and brought the bowls to the table. Samantha lit the candles. Soon Len, his jacket back on, entered with a platter of turkey. Beth followed with another. Ian popped open a bottle of chilled champagne and poured the bubbly liquid into each of the glasses at the table.

When they were all seated, Ian raised his glass and made a toast. "In thanks for the good year we've had at Whitebrook, for good health, good friends, and a toast to Cindy, who we welcome to our family. Happy Thanksgiving!"

The glasses clinked together, and Cindy felt tears in her eyes. They were so kind, so loving! How lucky she was!

On Saturday a car Cindy didn't recognize came down the Whitebrook drive and parked. She was pushing a wheelbarrow of dirtied bedding out to the muck pile, which when aged for a year fertilized the vegetable garden Beth was creating behind the cottage. Cindy paused and studied the two men who got out of the car. Because of her problems with the Child Welfare Department, she always felt anxious when a strange car drove into the yard.

She didn't recognize the men, though. One was in a business suit, the other in jeans and a down jacket. Mike came out of his office and greeted them. With a sigh of relief, Cindy decided their visit had nothing to do with her and continued on to the muck pile. When she returned with the empty wheelbarrow, Mike, her foster father, and the men were still standing outside Mike's office. Cindy wheeled the barrow back inside the training stable building and left it near the tack room. All the stalls had been mucked for the day. She was heading back down the aisle when the men came into the barn.

Her foster father walked over to her. "These are the men from the estate. They want to take a look at Glory. Can you bring him out?" His eyes held an apology. "I'd do it myself, but he's more relaxed with you."

"What do they want?" Cindy asked frantically. "Are they taking him away?"

"No. One of the men is the attorney. The other is a bloodstock appraiser. They only want to set a value on Glory for the estate records."

That was bad enough, Cindy thought as she walked stiffly to Glory's stall, took his lead shank from the hook outside, and unlatched the door. She felt chilled as she clipped the shank to his halter and led him out. "It's okay, boy. There're just some people who want to look at you."

Glory snorted uneasily when Cindy led him down the aisle and he saw the men. His nostrils widened as he scented the air. By now he knew Mike and Ian, but he didn't know the other two men, and it was obvious to Cindy that the colt didn't want to have anything to do with the strangers.

He stopped in his tracks, snorted, and pranced uneasily. "Come on, boy," she whispered. "It's okay. No one's going to hurt you."

Glory's ears flicked in her direction, but still he hesitated, then pawed the ground.

The men came toward them. Cindy took a firmer grip on Glory's lead shank and laid a comforting hand on his shoulder. The man in the down jacket raised his brows. "Nice-looking animal," he said in surprise.

"You didn't think he would be?" the other man asked.

"I had my doubts."

Mike, Ian, and the two men were only a few feet away now. Ian made introductions. "Cindy, this is Mr. Worth, a bloodstock agent, and Mr. Skoglund, the attorney representing the estate. This is my daughter, Cindy, who found the horse."

The men nodded to her. Although Cindy felt a surge of happiness to hear Ian refer to her as his daughter, she was filled with misgiving. Glory eyed the strangers uneasily. Cindy could feel his muscles quiver under her hand. She wanted to tell him that it was okay, but it wasn't!

The man in the parka, Mr. Worth, slowly walked around the colt. His eyes made a careful inspection. Glory snorted again and tried to twist his head around to see what the man was doing.

"Nice conformation," Worth said. "Strong hind-quarters, deep girth, good legs." He went to Glory's head and checked his teeth and tattoo, then checked the colt's feet. Glory didn't like the stranger touching him, and Cindy had to hold the colt's head firmly. "Can you walk him for me?" the agent asked.

Cindy looked over to her foster father. "Why don't you take him out and walk him around the yard, Cindy?"

Unhappily, Cindy followed his instructions. "Come on, big guy. Let's go out." Glory followed her willingly, eager to get outside, yet he eyeballed the attorney and agent as they passed the men.

With leaden steps, Cindy took Glory to the stable yard and walked the colt in a circle. The men watched intently. The agent made notes on the clipboard he carried and spoke to the attorney. Cindy strained to hear what he was saying, but the men were too far away. This was the only time Cindy wished with all her heart that Glory would make a bad impression. Finally her foster father motioned for her to bring Glory over.

"I'd say that he's the best of the lot," the agent told the attorney.

Cindy felt sick hearing the comment. Her chances for keeping Glory seemed to be slipping further away.

"Of course, he's untried," the agent added, "and he'll be going into the auction ring as an unraced three-year-old, which could be a disadvantage. At least he's received some training, and you can provide the records from the training stable."

Cindy noticed glumly that the attorney was looking more and more pleased. "To think that if you hadn't found him, the estate wouldn't have known he was missing," he said to Mike.

Cindy wondered ruefully if honesty was always the best policy. If Mike and Ian hadn't reported finding Glory, she wouldn't be losing him now. She should have kept him hidden away forever—though she knew that wouldn't have been possible.

"I'll be in touch," Mr. Skoglund continued. "A van will be sent over a few days before the auction to pick him up. You're still agreeable to boarding him here? He seems to be getting very good care."

Mike nodded. "He's getting excellent care."

"You'll be reimbursed for all your expenses, of course." The lawyer extended his hand to Mike and Ian, then he and the agent turned toward their car.

Cindy had to bite back her tears. Their showing up made Glory's imminent departure seem even more real. Her foster father came over and put an arm around her shoulders. "I know it's hard for you, Cindy. I wish there were an alternative, but there isn't at the moment."

Mike's expression was sympathetic too. "Skoglund did say that the estate would be paying a several-hundred-dollar finder's reward. That reward goes to you."

Cindy was grateful, but what was a reward in comparison to Glory? She knew she couldn't buy him for several hundred dollars.

She spent the next hour in Glory's stall, grooming him, talking to him, with Imp and Jeeves keeping them company. "You didn't like those men any more than I did, did you, boy? I can't blame them, though. It's not their fault that you have to be sold, but having them look at you like they did . . . like you were a piece of furniture or something! It made me sick. They didn't care about you or your future. All they were interested in was how much money you'd make them! It's not fair!" With the back of her hand, Cindy swatted a tear off her cheek. "Oh, Glory, we've got to do something!"

Glory huffed softly and touched his nose to her shoulder. He didn't understand her words, but he sensed her mood and her misery.

Cindy pressed her cheek against the colt's and tightened her jaw. "We'll find a way, boy. I'm not going to lose you."

8

When Cindy left Glory's stall, the first thing she did was call Heather. She told her friend about the agent and the lawyer's visit.

"That must've been awful for you, Cin!" Heather exclaimed.

"It was, but it made me decide that we have to work fast. Do you think you could come over this afternoon and ride with me? You could spend the night."

"I'll ask my parents. They're going out in a few minutes, but I could ride my bike over. Are you sure Beth and Ian don't mind me spending the night so often?"

"They like having you come over. They want me to have friends."

"Okay, hold on, I'll ask."

Cindy paced as she waited for Heather to get back on the phone. She was already planning their ride for that afternoon—a two-mile canter, then a long trot back over the lanes. She'd read in her books that long cross-country rides helped build muscle and stamina. And if Heather could spend the night, they could ride again on Sunday for an even longer distance.

Heather came back on. "They said fine. I'll leave in about ten minutes, okay?"

"Yes! I'll get the horses tacked while I'm waiting."

Heather lived several miles away, closer to downtown Lexington, but it wouldn't take her long to get to Whitebrook on her bike. Cindy went out to the paddock to collect Bo Jangles and bring him into the barn. Ashleigh was coming out of Mike's office and waved and smiled. "Going for a ride?" she asked.

Cindy nodded.

"A good day for it. I hope this weather lasts. Have fun."

"We will," Cindy called, feeling a twinge of guilt. No one suspected what she and Heather were doing, and Cindy was sure they wouldn't approve if they did know. She couldn't let that stop her, though. Glory's future was more important.

By the time Heather arrived, rosy cheeked and breathless, Cindy had the horses tacked and ready to go. The girls put on their hard hats before leading the horses out. Glory pranced out of the barn eagerly. Cindy patted his shoulder before leading him to the mounting block. Grabbing a handful of his mane, she put her foot into the stirrup and swung up into the saddle. The colt was so tall, Cindy needed to use the block to reach the stirrup. The air was crisp, but that only seemed to invigorate the horses.

As they set off down the lane away from the stable yard, Cindy explained to Heather what she wanted to do.

"Sounds good to me," Heather said. "What route do you want to take?"

"I can't take him on the trails through the woods, but if we head out past the shed, we can follow the lanes all the way to the far side of the property, then circle around behind the back paddocks. When we get to the edge of the woods, we can turn around and trot back. I've ridden that way with Sammy, and I think it's about two miles each way."

Heather grinned. "Ready when you are."

When they reached the lane leading past the shed where Cindy had hidden Glory, they reined the horses left and urged them into a slow canter. Glory was full of energy, and Cindy had to keep a firm grip on his reins to prevent him from lengthening his stride. She was afraid of pushing him too hard and overworking him. From what the books said, that would do far more harm than good.

Because Cindy was keeping the pace slow, Heather and Bo were able to keep up, although Bo had to work harder than Glory to do so. At that moment, with Glory striding smoothly over the grass, Cindy was able to forget her worries and just enjoy the thrill of riding the beautiful colt. She had only been riding for six months, yet she felt so at home in the saddle. Hearing the pound of Glory's hooves and feeling his powerful muscles bunch and relax beneath her seemed so familiar—as if she had ridden forever.

Cindy glanced over to Heather and saw that

Heather's face was glowing too. "How're you doing?" Cindy asked.

"Great!"

They reached the western boundary of the property, then cantered onto the lane to the right, which ran parallel to the property line. Beyond were the paddocks of a neighboring farm. Cindy never went near the eastern boundary of Whitebrook. It was on that neighbor's farm that she had discovered Glory. The men who had stolen him were gone, arrested and in jail, but the place still gave her the creeps, and seeing it again might upset Glory.

Cindy paid careful attention to Glory as they continued cantering. She watched for any signs that he was tiring, in which case she would slow him down. He was still moving easily, though, and had barely worked up a sweat. She glanced over to see how Bo was doing, but Bo was tough and used to hard work.

Cindy saw the beginning of the woods ahead. The bare-branched trees seemed stark against the blue sky. The two miles had gone faster than she'd expected, but as they approached the end of the lane, she began to rein Glory in. Heather did likewise until both horses had slowed to a trot, then a walk. Cindy circled Glory at a walk and felt his neck. He was damp, but not lathered. She looked over to Bo Jangles. "How does he feel?" she asked Heather. "If you think he's too tired, we can walk back."

"He feels fine."

"So does Glory," Cindy said, and she smiled as the colt snorted and tossed his head, eager to get going again. "Tomorrow we'll go farther, maybe try cantering them over some of the hilly paddocks. The book says that helps build stamina. Okay, Glory, let's head back."

The trip home took longer at a trot, but by the time they reached the stable yard, both horses had cooled down and showed no signs that the girls had given them a fairly rigorous workout. Cindy was glad of that because Samantha, Ashleigh, and Ian were in the training stable when she and Heather led the horses in to untack them.

"You both have roses in your cheeks," Ashleigh said. "Have a good time?"

"We sure did," Heather replied. "I really want to thank you for letting me borrow one of your horses, Ashleigh."

"We're glad to do it. I would have been miserable when I was your age if I hadn't had a horse to ride. In fact, I remember losing riding privileges for a month because I failed math. I thought it was the end of the world!"

They all laughed.

"Are you guys going to come out and watch the workouts tomorrow morning?" Samantha asked.

Heather looked at her in surprise. "You work the horses on Sundays?"

"When we need to, and we have to take advantage of the good weather and get as much work in as we can before it gets icy and the ground freezes."

"We'll be there," Cindy said. Watching the workouts had become even more important to her.

The next morning both girls hopped out of bed at six when the alarm went off. With the shorter days, workouts started later than they did in the summer. They were dressed in minutes and hurried downstairs. Each of them grabbed an apple from the bowl on the table, then, bundled up in parkas, they hurried out to the training oval. The others were already there.

Vic held one horse while Mike checked its saddle girth. Ian led another from the training stable. He'd thrown a sheet over the horse's back to keep him warm while he waited his turn to work. Mike gave Ashleigh a leg into the saddle of the first horse and spoke quickly to her.

Cindy hurried closer so that she could hear. "Take him around twice at a slow gallop," Mike told Ashleigh. "If he's not blowing, pick up the pace a little for another half mile, but don't breeze him."

Ashleigh nodded and headed the horse through the gap onto the track. Cindy recognized the horse as one that Mike boarded and trained for another owner. The horse had only been at the farm for a month or so. Samantha joined Cindy and Heather at the rail to watch the workout.

"Why did Mike want Ashleigh to work him like that?" Cindy asked the older girl.

"Because the colt still needs conditioning, and slow works will help. Mike doesn't want to work him too hard too soon, but if he's still moving easily after two miles, then Mike feels confident in asking a little more of him."

"Ashleigh can tell that while she's riding him?" Heather asked.

"Oh, definitely. You know when you've got a tiring or laboring horse under you."

They continued watching the workout—Cindy studying the horse's movements. They lapped the track once, then again. As Ashleigh and the colt neared the end of the second lap, Cindy thought she saw a change in the horse's strides. They seemed less fluid, more uneven, as if he were laboring to keep up the pace. Cindy wondered if she were imagining it. But as Ashleigh galloped the horse past the last marker post, she immediately rose higher in the stirrups and began pulling the horse up, letting him canter a dozen yards up the track before turning him.

"I was right!" Cindy said excitedly as Ashleigh rode the horse off the track.

Samantha smiled over to her. "You noticed he was starting to labor? Good for you! My turn to ride. See if you can figure out Dad's strategy on your own." Samantha strode over to her father, who had pulled the sheet off his horse. She snapped the chin strap of her helmet in place and prepared to mount. Cindy and Heather hurried over to listen.

"I want to clock him," Ian said. "Gallop him through the half, then breeze him out four furlongs." He gave Samantha a leg into the saddle, and she quickly settled herself and adjusted her grip on the reins. She winked at Cindy and Heather before she rode out onto the track.

"Okay," Heather said quietly to Cindy. "First of all, tell me what breeze means."

"Fast gallop—like you were in a race."

"Then this horse must be in pretty good condition."

Cindy nodded and chewed her lip thoughtfully. "If my foster dad is clocking him, then he must be getting close to racing him."

"You think?"

"Ashleigh and Samantha always clock Shining the last few workouts before she races."

"I remember reading something about that in one of the books you borrowed—something about fractions?" Heather frowned in confusion.

"Yeah. It's good if a horse can average twelve seconds per furlong. That's an eighth of a mile." She did some quick math in her head. "So if Samantha's breezing him four furlongs, then a good time would be forty-eight seconds."

"What if they go faster than that?"

Cindy smiled. "I think my foster dad would be pretty happy. I can remember Ashleigh shouting 'Twenty-two and change' after Sammy had breezed Shining a quarter mile before one of her races. She and Sammy were thrilled."

They stopped talking and watched. Samantha had finished warming up her mount and was approaching the marker pole. When they came alongside, Samantha urged her mount into a relaxed gallop. They still seemed to be flying as they swept past the girls and headed into the first turn. They continued at that pace to the half-mile marker. Then Samantha crouched lower over her mount's withers and kneaded her hands along his neck, signaling him to pick up the pace. His strides lengthened, and now they truly seemed to be flying. Samantha continued urging him on with her hands. Cindy glanced over and saw her foster father click the button on his stopwatch at the quarter pole, then at the eighth pole. He hit it for the last time as Samantha swept past the mile marker. Samantha immediately stood in the stirrups and pulled her mount up.

"How fast do you think they were going?" Heather asked.

"I'm not sure. I have trouble guessing. I've watched some horses that looked like they were going incredibly fast and weren't, and others that didn't seem to be going that fast at all and they were. I think it has something to do with the length of a horse's stride. Long-striding horses cover more ground without seeming to be going that fast."

"That's a plus for Glory, then!" Heather said with a grin. "He definitely has long strides. I should know from trying to keep up with you."

"Let's see if we were right about the workout."

Samantha had dismounted, and Vic led the horse she'd been working off toward the stable yard to cool him out. Samantha and her father talked for a moment. Ashleigh was already up in the saddle of the next horse to be worked, Rocky Heights. Cindy had seen him worked many times before. Mike had bought the gelding at the same auction where he'd bought Shining. He had been in nearly as bad shape as Shining, but now he was winning quite a few allowance races for Mike, and he was scheduled to be shipped to Florida for the Gulfstream winter races.

Samantha walked over to the girls. "Okay, let's hear your analysis, then I'll tell you if you're right or not."

Both girls started talking at the same time, then Heather nodded to Cindy that she should go first.

"I think because you breezed him, he's getting ready for a race. That would mean he's in top condition."

"Right so far," Samantha said, smiling. "What about the breeze? Do you think he passed the test?"

Cindy was more uncertain here. "You looked like you were flying, but . . ." She made a decision. "Yes, he did."

"Just barely," Samantha said. "He breezed the first quarter in twenty-four, three eighths in thirty-six, but he only did the half in forty-nine. Not very impressive for a horse who's going to run in an allowance race in four days. In fact, Dad's having second thoughts about entering him. He's thinking of giving him another week before he races."

"It's hard to tell how fast a horse is going without a stopwatch," Heather protested.

"It is. It takes a lot of practice and experience before you can trust your eye, but you guys have done pretty well so far," Samantha said. "One more question. Do you think he's a sprinter or a distance horse?"

"What's the difference?" Heather asked. Cindy thought she knew, but she was glad Heather had asked.

"A sprinter is a horse who excels over short distances—a mile or less, but usually six or seven furlongs. They generally have a powerful burst of speed up front, out of the gate, but they can't keep it up beyond a mile. A distance horse is at its best at a mile and a sixteenth or longer. They often kick in late and make a powerful closing drive or sit just off the pace, then find another gear before the finish. Shining is a distance horse. Blues King is a sprinter. Mike retired him this fall, but Cindy saw him race at Saratoga."

"Then the horse you rode must be a sprinter," Heather said. "He ran faster at the beginning of the breeze than at the end."

"True, but there's one clocking I didn't give you guys. He galloped out the mile in very good time. He slowed down at the end of the breeze, but his overall time for the mile was decent."

"This is so confusing," Heather said.

Cindy felt bewildered too. "But how can you tell from workouts whether a horse is a sprinter or a distance horse?"

"You can't sometimes, until after they've raced. Horses develop as they grow. A two-year-old sprinter could turn out to be a three-year-old distance horse." Samantha suddenly sobered. "Actually, I think they should do away with two-year-old racing. Two-year-olds aren't even full grown, and because the official birth date of all Thoroughbreds is January first, some two-year-olds are up to five months older than others. Expecting them to race and win is asking too much. It's too stressful. We push them too hard, and they end up breaking down before they're three. Too many winners of the big two-year-old races have been injured and couldn't race again."

"Whitebrook trains and races two-year-olds," Cindy said.

"Yes, but that's economics. Not many owners or

trainers can afford to hold over their two-year-olds for the following season. It's hard making a living in the Thoroughbred business, and a trainer is under tremendous pressure to get two-year-olds out on the track. There are tons of two-year-old races, Breeders' Cup awards, and you have to think of the expense of feeding, training, and vet bills. It's a luxury to hold back a horse when it's not earning its keep. Of course Dad and Mike only race the two-year-olds they feel are mature enough and ready to race. I can't say the same for a lot of owners and trainers." Samantha shook her head. "Anyway, that's all kind of serious for this conversation." She glanced over her shoulder. "And I've got another horse to work. Catch you guys later."

Samantha hurried off, and Cindy and Heather stayed to watch the rest of the four workouts. Basically, the horses being worked were all headed to Florida for the winter races. Horses like Shining, who had worked hard through the summer season, were being given time to rest.

"Do you understand all this?" Heather asked when the girls headed back to the cottage for breakfast.

"I'm more confused now than I was before," Cindy admitted.

"So what are we going to do?"

"Just keep working Glory to get him in shape. I don't think there's any way we can be sure he's going to be a good racehorse. But I feel it. I feel like he's going to be!"

"So do I," Heather said. "Let's go three miles today."

9

THEY WORKED GLORY FOR THREE MILES THAT DAY, BUT THEY changed their route, cantering the horses back and forth over a large, hilly paddock. The longer and tougher workout didn't seem to bother Glory. He was more sweated up than the day before, but he wasn't blowing in exhaustion, and Cindy was encouraged.

"You should be happy about today," Heather said as they trotted the horses back to the stable yard.

"I am, but there's just one problem. I really should take Glory out every day, but I'm not allowed to take him out alone, and you can't come over every day."

"No," Heather said, frowning in thought. "I could come over a couple of days. Couldn't you take him out for long walks by yourself? Or you could work him on the longe line."

Cindy's face brightened. "Why didn't I think of that? There's one small problem, though. I've watched horses being longed, but I've never tried it myself."

"Ask Sammy to teach you. Glory needs exercise. No one should mind if you work him on the longe line."

"Right," Cindy said. "I'll ask her tonight." Then she had a less cheerful thought. "Heather, I was just remembering how the men who stole him treated him on the longe line—how they hit him with the whip until he reared."

"But they were mean to him when they rode him, too, and he lets you ride him," Heather reasoned. "I think he knows you'd never hurt him."

Cindy hoped Heather was right.

Samantha willingly agreed to teach Cindy. "It's a great thing for you to learn," Samantha told her. "If you know how to longe, you can help out with some of the early training. Let's see, I'll be home from classes early tomorrow afternoon. We can start then."

Cindy beamed. "Thanks."

She passed on the good news to Heather the next day at school, and that afternoon she rushed out to the stables to find Samantha and get Glory.

Samantha was in the stable office and told Cindy that she would meet her at Glory's stall. As usual, Glory was glad to see Cindy. He nickered an eager greeting and waited for his carrot. While he munched, Cindy removed his blanket and gave him a quick brushing. By the time she was done, Samantha had arrived at the stall carrying a bridle, longe line, and whip. She set down the line and whip outside the stall, then carried in the bridle.

"This is a longeing bridle, or cavesson," she told Cindy. "You can see where the longe line is clipped onto the noseband. This gives you more control, and you don't have to worry about dangling reins. It goes on the same as a regular bridle." She handed it to Cindy, who slipped it over Glory's head and buckled the nose and cheek straps.

"Okay, let's take him out to the yearling ring," Samantha said. "I'll explain the rest of the equipment there."

Glory followed Cindy willingly, pricking his ears and sniffing the air as they stepped out of the barn. They followed Samantha to the enclosed ring behind the barns, which was used primarily to school yearlings and other young horses. The six-foot fence surrounding most of the ring helped to prevent the young horses from being distracted by other stable activity.

They entered the enclosure, and Samantha clipped the longe line to the ring on the top of the noseband of the bridle. Glory flicked his ears and gave a snort of uneasiness.

"I don't know if I told you, Sammy," Cindy said quickly, "but the men who stole him hit him with the whip when they longed him. He was terrified."

"I remember, and we'll go slow so we don't frighten him. You've watched the yearlings longed, so you know the principle. You want to get the horse moving around you in a big circle at an even pace. I'll show you, then let you have a try." Samantha looped the longe in her right hand and steadied it with her left. "Since he has bad memories of this, I think it would be a good idea for you to walk at his head and guide him through the first few circles. Gradually, as he gets going, I'll let out more and more of the longe so that he's moving in a wider circle. Eventually I'll keep his pace steady by flicking the whip on the ground behind him. But I don't want to use the whip yet. We'll start counterclockwise. Go to his outside and lead him by the side of his noseband. Once he's moving, gradually remove your hand but keep walking alongside. Got it?"

Cindy nodded and did as Samantha had instructed.

"Let's go then, at a walk."

"Come on, Glory, let's walk," Cindy said.

"Good," Samantha called. "Lead him in a wider circle as I let out the longe. Good. Keep going. Don't talk to him. He has to learn to pay attention to the person in the center."

They circled Samantha twice, then Cindy gradually released her grip on the noseband. Glory kept moving forward. Cindy could see Samantha nodding. "Okay, Cindy, gradually step away."

Cindy did, and Glory kept going.

"Let's trot, Glory," Samantha called. "Come on, pick up the pace."

Glory continued at a walk. Samantha motioned to Cindy to get the whip. Cindy did so, feeling a touch of uncertainty, but Glory had been doing well so far. Maybe he'd forgotten his past bad experiences. Carrying the whip close to her side, she approached Samantha from behind so the colt couldn't see what she was carrying.

Samantha took the whip. "Stay here with me so you can see what I'm doing. Trot, Glory!" As Samantha called out the command, she flicked the long, slim whip, which looked a lot like a fishing pole. Its end snapped harmlessly into the dirt several feet behind Glory.

Glory's ears shot back at the sound. He let out a frightened squeal and bolted forward. Samantha was caught totally by surprise. She had to grab at the longe to keep Glory from pulling it from her hands. The horse plunged in a circle around the girls.

"Easy, easy, Glory," Cindy called, trying to stop her voice from trembling. The colt didn't respond. "What are we going to do?" Cindy whispered anxiously to Samantha.

"Keep talking to him. If he doesn't slow down, I'll pull him into a tighter circle so he has to change pace."

Cindy called out again. "Whoa, Glory. Easy, boy. Slow down. It's okay." She saw Samantha draw in on the longe, giving a few short, sharp pulls to get Glory's attention. Cindy's heart was in her throat, but she continued talking to the frightened horse. Samantha had managed to pull in about a quarter of the longe line. The circle was becoming too small for Glory to continue galloping. Finally he broke stride and slowed to a canter, but the colt was still in a state of panic. Samantha continued pulling in the longe, but to Cindy it seemed to take forever for Glory to respond. At last, tossing his head and giving a ragged snort, he dropped to a trot.

Cindy expelled a huge breath of relief.

"Guess we won't try the whip for a while," Samantha said tightly. "Give him a minute to settle down."

The colt was trembling when he slowed to a walk. Cindy quietly went over to him. "You poor boy. We didn't mean to frighten you. I could kill those men for what they did."

Samantha walked up beside them. "Whew! That's the most exciting longeing session I've ever had." She laid a hand on the colt's shoulder. "Easy, big guy. I'm sorry I frightened you."

"What do we do now?" Cindy asked uncertainly.

"We'll come up with another strategy. Let's walk him while I think. In the opposite direction," she added.

Cindy turned Glory, and they walked slowly while Samantha considered. "He has to learn to respond to voice commands so a whip isn't necessary. I've got an idea. We'll longe him under tack. Keep walking him, and I'll get his regular bridle and saddle. I don't want to put him through much more today, but I don't want to end on a bad note, either."

Samantha hurried off. Cindy walked Glory and spoke soothingly to him. He seemed to have calmed down, but Cindy was concerned. She already had so little time to condition him. She didn't need another obstacle.

Samantha returned with saddle and bridle, and they quickly changed Glory's tack. Samantha explained what she wanted to do. "You ride, and I'll work the longe. Do the same as before. Start at a walk, then move up to a trot. Use your regular aides to get him to change gaits, but when you do, say the command out loud, and always use the same command words—walk, trot, and canter. Ready to try?"

Samantha had brought a hard hat too, and Cindy put it on. She felt some nervous flutters in her stomach. She'd never been afraid while riding Glory, but now she was uneasy. What if he bolted like he did before? She tried to convince herself that wouldn't happen.

When Cindy was settled in the saddle, Samantha clipped the longe line to Glory's bridle and backed away a half-dozen paces. "Okay, start him walking," she said.

Cindy tapped her heels against Glory's side. "Walk, Glory," she said firmly. The colt instantly obeyed as he always obeyed her physical commands. Samantha let out line as they continued walking in an ever larger circle.

"Ask him to trot," Samantha told her.

Cindy collected rein, tightened her legs on the girth, and pressed her seat deeper in the saddle. "Trot, Glory." He smoothly changed gaits. Cindy breathed a sigh of relief and began posting, lifting her weight when Glory lifted his outside shoulder.

"Good," Samantha called. Cindy could hear the smile in the older girl's voice, but she kept her eyes forward in the direction they were going. They circled Samantha several times at an even trot, then Samantha said, "Try to get him to canter."

Cindy swallowed, but tightened her left rein and pressed with her leg. "Canter, Glory." Again Glory understood her physical commands and moved smoothly into a canter. After they'd made two circuits, Samantha called, "I think that's enough for today. End it on a good note before he gets tired. Pull him back into a trot, then a walk."

Cindy did, voicing each command. She stopped Glory, and Samantha came toward them, gathering up the longe line as she did. She was grinning, and now that they were finished, so was Cindy. She patted Glory's neck. "Good boy. Excellent!"

Glory huffed his appreciation. Cindy dismounted and pulled up the stirrup irons.

"That's better," Samantha said. "A few more sessions like that and he should follow the voice commands without a rider. But keep reinforcing them. Whenever you ride him, every time you change gaits, call out the command."

Cindy nodded. "Thanks, Sammy. I really appreciate your helping me."

Samantha smiled back and squeezed Cindy's shoulder. "Anytime. We want to make a good horsewoman out of you, don't we? Want to try again Friday afternoon? I don't have any late classes."

"Yes!"

"Good. See you in the house for dinner."

Cindy was feeling much more optimistic as she led Glory back to the stable to put him in crossties and untack him. After she'd put his tack away, she felt his belly inside his legs to see if he was still hot and needed further cooling out. She decided to be safe rather than sorry, and since it was already getting dark outside, she led him up and down the long barn aisle for several minutes before sponging him, drying him, and giving him a good grooming. She buckled his blanket in place, then led him into his stall and went to get his evening feed. She hugged his neck before she left for the house. "Thanks, boy, and please don't be scared anymore. I wouldn't ever do anything to hurt you. I'm going to go call Heather and tell her the good news."

On Tuesday afternoon, Cindy clipped a lead shank to Glory's halter and took him out on the lanes. They walked for more than a mile, then she started jogging alongside him, encouraging him to trot. She could barely keep up with the colt's long strides and was breathless when they stopped, but she was satisfied the time had been well spent.

The weekly Pony Commando lesson was scheduled for the following afternoon. Cindy hadn't said a word to Heather about the free lesson Tor would be giving her, although Samantha had told Cindy that Tor had agreed. Cindy couldn't wait to see Heather's reaction.

No one said anything to Heather until after the lesson was over and they were untacking the ponies. Tor walked up, then said smilingly to Heather, "I hear you'd like to learn to jump?"

Heather looked up at him in surprise, her cheeks flushing. "Well, yes. I'd love to, but—"

"Sammy and I would like to do something to thank you for helping with the Commandos. How would you like a free riding lesson once a week after the Commando session?"

Heather's jaw literally fell open. She glanced over to

Cindy, but Cindy just shrugged with pretended innocence. Heather turned back to Tor. "You mean it?" she asked breathlessly.

"I wouldn't ask if I didn't."

"But . . . I mean—you're so busy. . . ."

Samantha intervened. "We want to do this for you in thanks for volunteering to help with the Commandos. Yvonne's already tacked up one of the stable horses. Are you ready?"

As Samantha spoke, Yvonne came down the aisle, leading a bay filly.

Heather looked from one smiling face to another, then looked over to the filly. Suddenly a smile lit her face, and her eyes sparkled. She nodded mutely to Samantha's question. "I don't know how to thank you," she said throatily.

"You don't have to thank us," Tor said. "This is our way of thanking you."

"I—I didn't bring my hard hat."

"There are spares in the tack room. One should fit you."

Heather turned to Cindy and grinned. Cindy winked back. Then Heather took a hesitant step toward Yvonne and the filly. "What's her name?" she asked, stroking the filly's nose.

"Sasha," Yvonne told her. "I've ridden her myself. She's a sweetheart and loves to jump."

Heather rubbed the filly's neck. "Hi there, Sasha. Are we going to be friends?" Then Heather turned to Cindy. "Will you stay and watch?" she asked excitedly.

"You bet."

Heather couldn't seem to stop grinning. "This is the most incredible surprise."

"Then let's head out to the ring," Tor said to her, "and get you started as a jumper."

With Tor leading the way, Cindy walked beside Heather and Sasha. Heather leaned over and spoke in Cindy's ear. "Thanks, buddy!"

Cindy lifted her brows. "But I didn't do anything."

Heather smiled and gave her friend a knowing look. "Sure."

10

All Heather could talk about the next day at school was jumping and what a great horse Sasha seemed to be. Cindy smiled at her friend's enthusiasm, understanding it well.

"Does this mean you won't have time to help me train Glory?" she asked teasingly.

"No, of course not," Heather said, offended. Then she saw Cindy's smile and grinned herself. "Okay, I get the message. Enough is enough, but I'm just so excited."

"You don't have to explain to me," Cindy said. "And I don't mind. Look how much I talk about Glory."

Over the next days Cindy continued working hard with Glory. She and Samantha spent Friday afternoon accustoming Glory to the longe line. He was beginning to obey Cindy's voice commands and work more smoothly. When Heather came over that weekend, she and Cindy took the horses for a canter over the trails, gradually increasing the distances they traveled. Glory seemed to revel in it, taking on every challenge, conquering it, and anticipating the next.

The weather didn't always cooperate. It rained heavily one day, and the air had a damp chill, but so far the temperatures had been milder than usual for early December, and there'd been no ice or snow. Cindy was thankful for that. She had so little time as it was. The Keeneland auction was January 6, less than a month away. Losing days to bad weather could be disastrous.

"What do you think?" Cindy asked Heather when they untacked and groomed the horses after their ride the following Tuesday. "Glory's muscles seem harder . . . or is it just my imagination?"

Heather studied the big gray. "He's thinner through the middle, but his chest and hindquarters seem bigger. The extra exercise has made a difference in Bo, too. Do you think we're getting there, Cin? How much more conditioning do you think Glory will need?"

Cindy wagged her head. "I don't know, but he doesn't seem tired when we finish up, even when we've worked him really hard. Maybe it's time to try galloping him."

Heather nodded. "But are you ready to try?"

"I've got to be. It's only two weeks until Christmas. We don't have much time left, and if we want to prove that he's good, we'll have to gallop him before we show him off to my foster father and Mike."

The girls exchanged an uncertain look. "Are we going to be able to do this?" Heather asked. "Are they going to laugh at us?"

"I don't know," Cindy said. "But I don't think they'll laugh." *They'll probably be furious with me instead*, Cindy thought.

The two girls stayed in Glory's stall, talking, until Heather's mother picked her up. It was dark by then. Cindy hurried into the cottage to get cleaned up before dinner. She waved to Samantha, Ian, and Beth, who were already gathered in the kitchen, then rushed upstairs to wash her hands and comb her hair.

Cindy was deep in thought when they all sat down at the table and began filling their plates. She looked up with her fork halfway to her mouth when Ian suddenly spoke to her. "We have something to tell you, Cindy," he said.

She lowered her fork. There was something unsettling in the tone of his voice.

"We all know how much you love Glory and how much you've done for the colt since you found him," he continued.

Cindy's stomach knotted. Was he going to tell her that they were coming to take Glory away?

"None of us want to see you lose him. Ashleigh and Mike and Beth and I talked it over and came up with a figure we thought we could afford. We made an offer to the estate." He hesitated. "It was a fair offer for an unraced colt and all we could afford." He gazed at Cindy as if he were trying to find the best way to say what he had to say. "Unfortunately, they turned us down."

Cindy stared at him. "You made an offer?"

"Yes. We offered them five thousand dollars, but their asking price is considerably higher. We just can't meet it."

"How much?" Cindy couldn't help asking.

"They want ten thousand for the colt."

Cindy's head was reeling. They cared enough about her that they had tried to buy Glory! But then the bad news sank in. The owner wanted more money. Cindy didn't know whether to thank her foster family or to cry.

"I'm sorry, Cindy," Ian said. "We wish we could have brought you happy news tonight. I didn't even want to tell you about our offer, but everyone else thought you were mature enough to know the truth. The attorney for the estate told us that the bloodstock agent, Worth, who you met that day, thought Glory was worth that much at auction. Of course, they're taking a risk. There are no guarantees that the bidding will go that high. I told Skoglund that, but he said the estate would be willing to take the chance. He and Worth felt there were buyers out there who would realistically pay their asking price."

Cindy swallowed. She felt overwhelmed. She remembered Samantha saying that Glory could be worth ten thousand dollars, but she hadn't entirely believed it. Now she was discovering that Whitebrook couldn't afford to pay more than half that amount.

Cindy felt on the verge of tears. It seemed even more hopeless now. Glory would never be hers.

She blinked, trying to forestall her tears and hide the emotions that were gripping her. She didn't want them to think she was ungrateful for all they'd done, but pain tightened her throat.

"Thank you . . . for trying," she said.

"I picked a bad time to tell you this," Ian said, sounding irritated with himself.

"It's okay," Cindy mumbled.

"No, it's not." He reached over and squeezed her hand. Cindy looked up and saw Samantha and Beth gazing at her with sympathy and understanding in their eyes. It was more than she could take. Before she broke down in sobs at the table, she excused herself and fled to her room. She closed the door behind her, then threw herself on her bed, pulled her pillow over her head, and sobbed.

She heard Beth and Ian knock on the door, but all she wanted was to be alone. She had always sought refuge in herself when things had gone wrong in the past. She'd had no one else to turn to then.

"I'm all right," she choked out. "Really. I just need to be alone for a while."

Eventually she heard them leave the hall. She heard them speaking as they went down the stairs. "I knew we shouldn't have said anything to her, Beth," Ian said anxiously. "It only made things worse."

"You're right," Beth answered. "This time I'll admit I misjudged the situation. I've always believed that the truth was better than lies or omission, but then, I never was a horse-mad girl."

Cindy couldn't hear the rest of their words, but a few moments later she heard a noise and lifted her head in time to see a note slipped under her door. It had to be

113

from Sammy. Miserable as she was, curiosity got the better of her. She went to the door and picked up the note. It was in Samantha's handwriting.

Cindy, we love you. I know how hurt you are, but don't give up hope. I never did. I wish I had some easy answers, but there still may be a way to keep Glory. Hang in there. I love you.

Your sister,
Sam.

Cindy refolded the note and held it in her hands, feeling touched. She was too miserable to think of teeth brushing or pajamas. She slipped the note under her pillow, then got in bed and pulled the covers over her head.

When she went downstairs in the morning, Cindy was still too upset to behave normally. She used the defense she had used so many times before, pretending that the conversation of the night before had never existed—withdrawing into herself.

She didn't think any of the McLeans were fooled, but they didn't question her.

The Pony Commandos were meeting that day after school. Heather was so excited about her lesson afterward that Cindy didn't have the heart to tell her about the refused offer for Glory. Why ruin her best friend's day too?

But as they were unsaddling the ponies after the

Commando class and Heather went off for her lesson with Tor, Mandy frowned and said to Cindy, "Something's wrong, isn't it? You look so sad. You hardly paid any attention during the lesson."

"I'll be okay, Mandy," Cindy said.

Mandy stared at Cindy, then shook her head. "Uh-uh. You look like I do when my legs don't get better fast enough."

Cindy heaved a sigh. She'd had no intention of telling anyone what was wrong, but suddenly she heard herself quietly telling Mandy.

"But that's not fair!" Mandy cried. "Those estate people don't care about Glory. They're only thinking of money."

"I know, Mandy, and so does everyone at Whitebrook, but there's nothing I can do anymore."

Mandy suddenly slapped her hand against one of her leg braces. "Oh, no? You keep telling me that I can get over these things. So why are you such a chicken?"

Cindy was caught by surprise. "I am not a chicken!"

"Then keep fighting! Don't give up yet. Hey, girl, you love that horse. If you try hard enough, you can get him. You can show them that Glory's worth ten thousand dollars."

Cindy felt embarrassed and humbled to have an eight-year-old tell her what to do. But Mandy's spirit revived hers too. "You're right, Mandy," she said with new determination. "I'm not going to give up. He is good, and I'm going to prove that he could be a great racehorse."

Mandy laughed and slapped her palm against Cindy's. "That's the way, Cindy!"

When Cindy finished putting away the last of the ponies, she stopped in the stable office to talk to Samantha about the upcoming Pony Commando Christmas show, which was less than two weeks away. Samantha was seated at Tor's desk, going through some papers.

"Sammy," Cindy said quietly. "I wanted to thank you for the note last night. I'm sorry if I seemed rude to everyone."

Samantha rose and put her arm around Cindy's shoulders. "No one thought you were rude, sweetie. We all knew how you were feeling. And maybe no one will be willing to pay what the estate wants."

Cindy managed a weak smile. She knew Samantha was trying to soften the blow, and she appreciated it. "I came by to see what you need me to do for the show."

"Well," Samantha said, returning to the desk. "I think I'm pretty well organized. Janet and Beth will take care of the refreshments. I'll really need your help on the morning of the show—Heather's too, if she's interested. All the ponies will have to be specially groomed— manes and tails braided with some bright ribbon. The kids love that, and it makes everything seem so much more Christmasy. And during the show, of course, we'll need you two to help the Commandos, like we do in a regular lesson. We're going to start with a walk, trot, canter class, then go to trotting over cavalletti and end the show with the two-fence jump."

"I'll be glad to help," Cindy said. "I'll talk to Heather

about helping too. I was just going in to watch the end of her lesson."

"Cindy, have you ever considered taking jumping lessons yourself?"

Cindy looked at Samantha in surprise. "I've thought of it, but I've been so busy."

"I just thought that maybe lessons would cheer you up and give you something to take your mind off Glory being sold."

"I'll . . . think about it." Cindy couldn't very well tell Samantha that she hadn't given up on Glory yet and was going to be spending what free time she had working the colt.

Samantha smiled. "Okay. I know today probably isn't a very good time to ask. You're feeling down. I'll see you later."

When Cindy entered the indoor ring, Heather had just finished trotting over cavalletti—poles raised no more than a few inches off the ground, a trotting stride apart—in her jump seat. Tor ended the lesson by having her practice jumping over a low crossbar.

"That's a good place to stop for today," he told her. "You're doing great."

Heather beamed him a smile. Her eyes were glowing. "Thanks, Tor!"

Tor returned her smile. "See you next week."

Cindy walked with Heather while she led Sasha around the ring to cool her out. "I'm sorry I didn't watch more of your lesson, but I was talking to Sammy about the Pony Commando show."

"That's okay," Heather said. "I'm less nervous when no one's watching."

"Sammy was wondering if you'd be able to help with the show."

"Sure," Heather said eagerly. "I love to watch the kids. They're all so excited already."

"I've got something to tell you," Cindy stated somberly. "Last night Ian and Beth told me that they and Ashleigh and Mike tried to buy Glory for me."

Heather turned quickly to Cindy, her face alight.

Cindy shook her head. "That was the good part. The bad news was that the estate turned them down. The estate has set a reserve of ten thousand and won't go below that unless no one bids that high at the Keeneland auction."

"Oh, no," Heather said sadly. "Did your foster parents tell you how much they offered?"

"Five thousand. It was all they could afford."

"That's not good news for us."

"I was ready to give up," Cindy said, "but I just got a pep talk from Mandy." Cindy smiled at the memory. "She told me I was a chicken if I didn't keep fighting."

Heather chuckled. "Yeah, I can picture her saying that. But what can you do, Cin? I mean, even if we keep training him, you know the people at Whitebrook can't afford to pay more than five thousand for him."

"But they might be willing to pay more if they thought he could be a good racehorse and earn money for the farm. They were trying to buy Glory as a pleasure horse for me."

"Are you sure they'd pay ten thousand if we prove he's good?" Heather asked.

"Pretty sure." Cindy hesitated for a moment. Actually she wasn't sure at all, but the more she thought about it, the more she thought that she was right. "The bloodstock agent who looked at Glory thought he would bring ten thousand at auction, proven or not." Suddenly Cindy frowned and chewed her lip. "I just hope that I'm right in thinking he's good, Heather."

"I think you are. Want me to come over tomorrow after school and help you give him another work?" Heather asked.

"Would you?"

"You bet."

11

AFTER CINDY AND HEATHER HAD TACKED UP THE HORSES THE next afternoon, they headed out under a leaden sky. Thankfully, the temperatures remained unseasonably warm, but Cindy knew that could change at any time.

Cindy glanced up at the clouds. "I hope it doesn't start raining until we're finished."

"When I went to get Bo's tack," Heather said, "Vic told me he'd just heard it was supposed to be rain mixed with snow."

"Oh, great. Snow is the last thing we need. We'd better get going before it starts."

They mounted and headed the two horses up the lane. Both Glory and Bo were in playful moods and took make-believe nips at each other's necks.

"Okay, guys, that's enough," Cindy said, reining Glory farther away from Bo. But she was smiling.

"I've got a surprise," Heather called over to Cindy. Heather was looking very pleased with herself.

120

"What kind of a surprise?" Cindy asked.

Heather reached into the pocket of her parka and pulled out a round silver object.

Cindy frowned as she tried to get a clear look. "What's that?"

Heather grinned. "A stopwatch. It's my dad's. He said I could borrow it. You can gallop him today, and I can clock you."

Cindy's eyes lit, but she was thinking, too. "We've only been guessing at the distances. How are we going to know if we've gone exactly a quarter of a mile?"

"I brought something else," Heather said confidently. "A tape measure. It's huge. My father uses it for measuring out distances on pieces of land for surveys and stuff."

"It's long enough to reach a quarter of a mile?" Cindy asked in disbelief.

"No, of course not. But we know how many feet there are in a mile, and if we divide that by four and measure out sections—"

Cindy nodded. "Gotcha. Let me think . . . there are 5,280 feet in a mile—right? I remember that, because we just had it in math class. So we divide by four. That's not easy in your head."

"I figured it out last night," Heather said. "It's 1,320 feet."

"Yikes, and we're going to measure all that out?"

"This is a hundred-foot tape measure," Heather said. "We mark the beginning. You take one end, and I'll take the other. We stretch the tape out its full length and then just keep moving forward thirteen times, then add twenty feet at the end. That should take about five minutes. Where do you want to gallop him? On that side lane where we cantered the first time?"

Cindy nodded. "That's about the flattest and straightest of the lanes, and it should be at least a quarter of a mile. I just hope I'll be able to get him to gallop and keep galloping. We'd better warm them up first. Let's canter them to the lane."

The girls urged the horses into a canter and moved smoothly over the grass toward their destination. At the end of the side lane they stopped the horses and dismounted, then tied their reins to the paddock fence rails. Heather pulled out her tape measure. Starting at the point where the lanes met, they measured out a quarter of a mile. It took a little longer than Heather's predicted five minutes. They marked the end of the quarter mile with a stick. Heather would stand there for the clocking.

They jogged back to the horses. "Well, I'm warmed up," Cindy said with a laugh. "I hope Glory is too." But her laughter hid the nervous tremor she felt inside. Could she get Glory to gallop the way Ashleigh and Samantha did with the horses they worked on the track? Would he have the kind of speed that was necessary? All the books said twenty-four seconds for the quarter mile was what trainers strove for on the training oval. But of course, this was her first time galloping Glory. They should allow for that.

Using one of the fence rails as a mounting block, Cindy got into Glory's saddle. It was a slightly heavier

English saddle than the ones used for the horses in training, but Cindy didn't think that would make much of a difference in her and Glory's performance.

Heather got into Bo Jangles's saddle. She pulled a red scarf from the neckline of her parka. "Do you think you'll be able to see this if I wave it from the other end?"

Cindy nodded. The scarf was bright, and there was nothing to obscure her view. "I hope it doesn't spook the horses," she said.

"I'm just going to hold it in the air, then drop my arm when it's time for you to start. I'm not going to wave it around or anything."

"Okay." Cindy checked the chin strap on her hard hat. "I'm going to walk him around a little to keep him limber until you get down to the end." She motioned to the first fence post along the lane. "I start him here, right?"

"Right. Here's hoping," Heather said, then trotted Bo off toward the stick that marked the end of the quarter mile.

Cindy walked Glory in a small circle. He seemed to know something was up—something different and exciting. He huffed out misty breaths into the cool air, arched his neck, and lifted his feet just a little higher.

"Yeah, boy," Cindy said, trying to control her nervousness. "We are going to do something different— important. I'm going to ask you to gallop . . . and ask you to put everything into it. I want you to show everyone that you could be a good racehorse. I don't want to lose you. I may not even be much help to you because I'm so nervous, but do you think you can?"

Glory gave a deep nicker. His ears had been cocked

123

back while she spoke. Now he ducked his chin and arched his neck and did a few prancing steps across the grass.

"I hope that means what I want it to mean," Cindy said. She looked down the lane and saw that Heather and Bo had reached the marker. Heather turned Bo and positioned him tight against the paddock fence, then pulled out her scarf and her stopwatch.

Cindy prepared herself. She brought Glory to the starting point, readjusted her hold on the reins and her position in the saddle, took several deep breaths, and waited. Glory's ears pricked forward, then back. He seemed to be waiting too, every inch of him alert for what might happen in the next seconds.

Heather raised her hand with the scarf, then lowered it.

Instantly Cindy kicked her heels against Glory's sides, kneaded her hands up his neck, giving rein, and shouted, "*Go!*"

Glory jumped out into a full-fledged gallop. Cindy was taken by surprise by the sudden speed. She had to grab handfuls of Glory's mane, together with the reins, to keep herself in the saddle. She pushed her heels farther down in the stirrups, keeping her toes high, for balance. Her heart was in her throat through the first half-dozen strides, but then she began to relax and concentrate only on Glory.

His long-striding gallop was like nothing she had experienced before. They seemed to be flying. Glory's mane whipped back at her face as she hunched over his withers. All she could hear was the sound of his pounding hooves and even breaths. Cindy realized the colt was enjoying himself, powering forward out of pure delight—increasing the pace on his own. His strides grew longer, and he seemed to be moving effortlessly. *This isn't work for Glory*, Cindy thought. *This is play. He loves it!*

Cindy looked ahead to Heather and Bo. She couldn't begin to guess how fast she and Glory were going, but they seemed to be approaching the marker with amazing speed. She would never forget this ride. It was the most incredible experience in her life.

Unconsciously she crouched lower and kneaded her hands along Glory's neck. He quickened his pace again. Then Cindy had a horrible thought. What if she couldn't stop him? What if he continued galloping across the meadow at the end of the lane and into the woods? She imagined them plunging out of control through the trees, Glory foundering over the rough path, catching his leg or stepping in a hole.

"No!" her brain cried. "Don't think of that now!"

Heather was only a few yards ahead. Cindy and Glory swept past, and Cindy, copying what she had seen Ashleigh and Samantha do during workouts, quickly rose in the stirrups and leaned her weight away from Glory's neck.

Glory didn't respond. He continued galloping headlong. "Whoa, boy, whoa!" Cindy cried, applying more pressure to the reins. Desperately she tried to think what to do. Then she remembered what Samantha had said during their first longeing session: Circle him. She had room in the large meadow. She drew on her right rein. Glory began to turn. Cindy maintained the pressure on the rein until they were galloping in a wide circle. She drew back on both reins. "Canter, Glory!" she commanded, as she did during their longeing sessions. "Come on, boy, please!" She was terrified not only for herself, but for the colt. If he got hurt because she was galloping him and lost control, how could she explain?

Finally, halfway through their second circle, Glory slowed his pace, then dropped back into a canter. Cindy nearly fainted with relief. She was trembling all over as they cantered the rest of the circle and rode back to Heather.

"You won't believe it!" Heather cried, holding up the stopwatch.

Cindy was still trying to recover from her fright. She pulled a ragged breath into her lungs as she drew Glory to a halt.

"Are you all right?" Heather asked with concern. "You're white as a ghost."

"I—I almost couldn't stop him," Cindy said breathlessly. "Couldn't you tell?"

Heather shook her head. "I thought you kept galloping him on purpose."

"No. He's the one who took me for a gallop. He didn't want to stop." Cindy's heart rate was slowly returning to normal. Glory tossed his elegant head, and Cindy gave him an unsteady pat on the neck. The colt obviously had no idea how much he'd frightened her.

"Well, here's the good news. He went the quarter mile in just under twenty-three seconds."

"He did?" Cindy exclaimed. "You didn't make a mistake?"

"Nope. I was careful to push the button just as you went by."

"Oh, wow!" Cindy said, feeling dazed. "He's even better than I expected. Those are the kinds of fractions Shining sets for the quarter mile." Then she had a chilling thought. "Heather, you don't think I worked him too hard—this is his first gallop."

"He doesn't look like you worked him too hard," Heather said with a smile. "He looks like he's ready to go another quarter mile."

"Not today," Cindy said quickly. "That would be much too much."

"I didn't mean today, but next time I come over."

Cindy reached down and felt Glory's neck. He'd worked up more of a sweat than usual, but that wasn't surprising. "We'd better take them for a long walk before we head back so he cools out."

Heather nodded, and the two girls set off. A moment later Heather gave a little laugh. "We did it, Cin. We trained a racehorse!"

Cindy knew they still had a lot more training to do before Glory was fully conditioned, but she returned Heather's grin. "We're on our way!"

Cindy was feeling cheerful that night as she finished up her homework and made plans for the days ahead. She would work Glory on the longe line the following afternoon. She was confident enough now to longe him on her own. And Heather was coming over on Saturday and would spend the night. Weather permitting, they would have two days to work Glory at a gallop again. She had already decided to try something new. Instead of putting Glory into a gallop at the beginning of the quarter mile, she would start him at a slow gallop along the opposite lane, then urge him to pick up speed when they reached the quarter-mile marker. She'd seen Ashleigh and Samantha do the same with so many horses that they had worked.

When Cindy finished her homework, she went downstairs for a snack. She was halfway down the staircase when she heard her foster parents talking in worried voices in the living room. She stopped in her tracks to listen.

"I thought we would have heard more about the adoption by now," Beth said. "We must have filled out a hundred forms, and we haven't even received an acknowledgment. And there were forms that were supposed to come back to us to be signed. You don't think that Lovell woman is holding things up, do you, Ian? She certainly took a dislike to us."

"I don't think she could do that," Ian said. "At least I hope not. After that debacle over the stolen watch that was never stolen, there's no reason to question Cindy's behavior . . . and her grades are good. In fact, her last report card amazed me—one B and the rest A's."

"She studies hard, Ian, and is so responsible about it. Neither of us ever has had to remind her to do her homework, in spite of the time she spends with the horses."

"I know. I sent a copy of the report card to the Child Welfare Department."

"Then why haven't we heard anything?" Beth asked. "Is it just red tape?"

"Maybe I'd better give our lawyer a call in the morning," Ian said. "He can tell us if this is normal."

"She's such a great kid, Ian, and she's been through so much. I can't bear to think of something going wrong with the adoption."

"It won't, Beth. The wheels of bureaucracy just move slowly."

But even Cindy could hear the question in his voice. She had suddenly lost her appetite for a snack. Was her adoption in jeopardy? Had something gone wrong? Had Lovell or the child welfare people changed their minds? So much of her future rested on their decisions, not hers! Cindy hated the whole lousy setup, but she was a minor. There was nothing she could do.

She quietly slipped back upstairs. She felt sick, and her stomach was tied in knots. All her thoughts over the last few weeks had revolved around Glory. She had forgotten her own uncertain situation. Now it came back to her like a bomb landing on her head.

She went to the single window in her bedroom and looked out into the night. What would she do if the McLeans weren't allowed to adopt her? She knew one thing for sure. She wasn't going to another foster home. She wasn't going to give up the first loving home she'd ever known.

Suddenly she thought of her parents and wondered

what they'd been like. She had been told so little. At first she was too young to understand, but when she had begun to ask questions, she really hadn't been given many answers.

They had been killed in a car accident when someone had cut them off on the interstate and they'd been forced off the road into a tree. They had been killed almost instantaneously, both of them crashing through the windshield because neither of them had been wearing seat belts. She, an infant, strapped into the backseat in her infant carrier, had survived.

Her parents' names were Jeff and Mary Lou Blake. They had both been twenty-four when they died. Nobody told Cindy much else, except that her full name was Cinthia Miranda Blake and that neither of her parents had any family that could take care of her.

Cindy looked out into the night sky and wondered about them. She didn't even know what they had looked like. She knew there had been photos, but they had gotten lost along the way—not by her, but by the child welfare people.

Somehow, without consciously realizing it, she had replaced the unknown faces of her real parents with the faces of Beth and Ian. They were what her parents would have been like if they were still alive.

Cindy turned from the window and tried to convince herself that it was too soon to panic. Ian and Beth would fight for her. She didn't doubt that for a minute.

12

CINDY DIDN'T SLEEP WELL AND WAS AWAKE BEFORE HER alarm went off at six. Before she got dressed, she went to the window and looked out. It had snowed during the night, but it was only a light dusting and would probably melt away before noon.

She didn't say anything to Ian or Beth about overhearing their conversation the night before, but as they all sat down to a quick breakfast, Beth noticed something was troubling Cindy.

She gave Cindy a worried look. "Are you feeling all right?"

"I'm fine," Cindy said, but Beth came over and felt her brow.

"Well, you don't seem to have a fever. But you look pale. Maybe you've been doing too much with the horses and your schoolwork and helping with the Pony Commandos."

Cindy definitely wanted to change the direction of Beth's thoughts. "No—no. I just didn't sleep very well last night."

Beth was still frowning with concern. Cindy noticed Samantha had looked in her direction too. "Okay, then," Beth said, returning to her breakfast. "I thought this weekend we could all go into Lexington to do some Christmas shopping."

"I invited Heather over," Cindy said quickly, thinking of her plans with Heather for working Glory that weekend. She didn't want to waste any of their precious time by going shopping.

"She can come too," Beth offered.

Ian saved the day. "Can we go tomorrow night instead? I've got a pretty heavy schedule lined up this weekend. Or you girls can go alone."

"It'll be more fun as a family trip," Beth answered. "Tomorrow night's fine with me. Cindy, Sammy?" She looked at them in question.

Cindy nodded eagerly. She glanced over to Samantha. "Actually, that would work out great," Samantha said. "Tor and his father are going to a horse association meeting, so I've got the night to myself."

"Then it's a date," Beth said in satisfaction.

Cindy quickly finished up her cereal, brought the bowl to the sink, and rinsed it. "I'll go out and help Len and Vic in the stables."

"Sammy and I will be out in a minute," Ian said.

Cindy collected her jacket from the rack in the front hall and hurried outside. The landscape looked beautiful dusted in white, but Cindy wasn't in a state of mind to appreciate it. In her mind she was counting the number of days until the auction in early January. If she concentrated on that and Glory, she wouldn't have time to dwell on her own situation.

As always, she went to Glory's stall first. He was waiting for her, eager for his breakfast. "Morning, handsome," Cindy said, a smile forming on her lips as she saw his elegant head over the stall door. He answered with a welcoming whicker.

Cindy unlatched the stall door and slipped inside, giving the colt a hug. Glory rested his muzzle on her shoulder for a moment, then gave her a meaningful nudge with his nose.

Cindy chuckled. "Yes, I know. You're hungry. I'll go get your breakfast."

Slipping out of his stall with his feed bucket, she hurried toward the feed room. She passed Vic in the aisle. He gave her a wide smile. "Pretty out there today, isn't it?"

"It sure is," Cindy replied, although snow was the last thing she wanted. In the feed room she measured out Glory's portion of grain and vitamins, then hurried back to his stall. As he thrust his nose eagerly into the bucket, she collected hay for his haynet and filled his water bucket. Then, while he continued eating, she took off his blanket and carefully checked him over, looking for any signs of soreness or swelling caused by yesterday's gallop. She certainly wasn't an expert, but to her unpracticed eye, Glory looked fine. There was no heat or swelling in his legs, he was moving easily, and he certainly hadn't lost his appetite. Satisfied, Cindy got his brushes and started grooming him.

She wished she could tell Glory about her worries of the previous night. He wouldn't understand her words, of course, yet talking would help. But the others were all coming into the barn, and she was afraid someone would overhear. Cindy decided she would talk to Heather at school.

When she had finished up with Glory, she gave him a last pat. "I'll see you this afternoon, big guy." Then Cindy left his stall to help with the other horses.

By seven forty-five, she had changed into her school clothes and was hurrying up the drive to catch the bus.

When they talked during lunch, Heather had been sympathetic, but told Cindy it was too soon to start worrying—to wait until she had heard what Ian had found out. She tried to cheer Cindy up by talking about Glory's great gallop and what they were going to do next. By the time she got home after school, Cindy was feeling better and couldn't wait to get out to the stable and longe Glory.

After she'd changed, Cindy grabbed an apple, pulled on her jacket, and headed for the barn. Ashleigh and Mike were in the office, but she didn't see Ian. His car was parked in front of the cottage, though, so he was around somewhere. Beth worked as an aerobics teacher in Lexington. Cindy collected the longeing bridle and longe line from the tack room, and after giving Glory a quick brushing, she led him out to the yearling ring.

Once they were in the ring, Cindy put everything from her mind but the colt's performance. He was so much better on the longe now, changing gaits smoothly on voice command. He seemed to have overcome his earlier fears.

Cindy circled him clockwise, then counterclockwise around her. She had read in the training books that it was important to change directions and not work a horse too long on one side and cause leg and muscle stress.

Since they would be galloping him tomorrow, Cindy didn't want to work the colt too hard that afternoon, and ended the session after half an hour.

She was leading the colt back toward his barn when she saw Ian at the other side of the yard, talking to Len. From the expression on his face, he didn't look upset. So maybe the news about her adoption wasn't bad.

Cindy was busy in the stables until dinnertime, but she felt an anxious little knot in her stomach when they all sat down and Ian looked in her direction.

"Cindy," he said, "I thought you should know that I talked to our lawyer about your adoption today. Beth and I were concerned that we hadn't heard anything."

Cindy waited, holding her breath, but Ian didn't sound upset.

"Our lawyer said it's normal for the proceedings to take a while, but he also said the authorities want to interview all of us again. I know," he added when he saw Cindy's dismayed expression. "I'm not looking forward to it any more than you are, but the lawyer says we shouldn't expect any problems. We have an appointment next Tuesday."

Cindy didn't want to face the social workers again. She was so nervous talking to them that her words never came out the way she intended. "What kind of questions are they going to ask?"

"I don't know," Ian replied, "but my guess is that they want to see how we interact together and how well you've adjusted in the last few months. Just be honest and be yourself."

"Is Mrs. Lovell going to be there?"

"Not if we have anything to say about it," Beth answered firmly. "We've told our lawyer that not only was the woman rude to all of us, but we feel she is unduly biased against you."

"Good," Cindy said softly. She didn't think she could get through another interview with Lovell without saying something rude that would jeopardize her chances.

"Our appointment is at three," Ian said. "We'll pick you up at school."

Cindy nodded and was glad when the conversation turned to the horses Ian was preparing for the trip to Florida in January. Cindy didn't want to think of the upcoming interview. Instead she let her thoughts wander to Glory and the following day's gallop.

As soon as they had finished dinner, they piled in the car and drove to the mall in Lexington. Shopping was definitely not one of Cindy's favorite pastimes, but shopping for Christmas presents wasn't so bad.

They split up in the mall and set a time and place to meet. Cindy and Samantha went in one direction, Ian and Beth in another. Cindy didn't have a lot of money to spend, but she found a silver horse pin for Heather. She'd already bought some pretty hair ties for Samantha at a crafts fair she'd gone to that fall with Heather and her family. She didn't have any ideas about what to get Ian and Beth, though. She asked Samantha.

"Why don't you go in with me?" Samantha suggested. "They've been wanting a new VCR for ages. I've already picked one out."

Cindy knew VCRs were expensive. "I've haven't got very much money, Sammy. I couldn't afford to pay half."

Samantha chuckled. "Of course not. I don't expect you to. Tor's chipping in too. Just give what you can afford."

"You're sure?"

"Positive."

"What about Ashleigh, Mike and Mr. Reese, and Len and Vic?" Cindy asked. "Should I get them something?"

"No, they won't expect it, but you could always give them a token gift, like your silver horseshoes."

Cindy smiled. For the Pony Commando summer show, she had painted old horseshoes in silver and given them to each of the riders. "I could do that," she said. "And decorate each one a little differently."

"So that problem's solved," Samantha replied

cheerfully. "Come help me pick out a sweater for Ashleigh."

When they met up with Ian and Beth at nine, Cindy was exhausted. She didn't understand why shopping tired her out so much. She could spend the same amount of time walking Glory over the lanes and not feel tired at all.

Everyone was secretive as they loaded their purchases into the trunk of the car. Cindy noticed Ian and Beth had at least a half a dozen big bags, and she couldn't help wondering if any of it was for her. Since she had never had any reason to anticipate Christmas or fun presents, she was taken by surprise by the bubble of excitement she was feeling now at the thought of Christmas morning.

When they arrived home, Cindy stopped in the kitchen for a snack, then said her good-nights and headed upstairs with her purchases. She quickly changed into her nightgown and brushed her teeth, then snuggled beneath the covers, thinking about Glory and their next day's workout.

13

HEATHER ARRIVED AT TEN THE NEXT MORNING, PEDALING HER bike down the Whitebrook drive. Cindy was waiting for her, and after they'd dropped Heather's backpack inside the cottage, they hurried out to the stables.

Cindy had already tacked up the horses.

"Did you hear any more about the adoption?" Heather asked as they led the horses from the barn.

Cindy repeated what Ian had told her. "But I'm scared about the interview," she added.

"After the way you've been treated, I don't blame you. But you said Lovell wouldn't be there."

"Yeah, that's one good thing. I still don't trust them, though. And why do they want another interview? What else could I tell them that they don't know already?" Cindy led Glory to the mounting block and got in his saddle.

"I don't know. Maybe they're just being extra careful. I'd be nervous about the interview too, but I think it will be different this time—less tense. I mean, they know you didn't steal Lavinia's watch. You said your foster father sent a copy of your last report card to them—they have to be impressed by almost straight A's. The interview's not until Tuesday. Try not to think about it and get bummed out."

Heather pulled herself up into Bo's saddle, and they headed the horses toward the lane between the paddocks. They kept them on a loose rein so the horses could extend their necks and work any kinks out of their muscles at a relaxed pace.

"You're right," Cindy agreed. "And now there's something more important to think about—Glory." She reached down to rub Glory's neck, and he gave a whicker of pleasure. They had left the barns behind, and Cindy suggested they trot the horses.

"Do you still want to try a longer gallop today?" Heather asked.

"Yes. I think he's ready, and we won't know if he's got any stamina unless he can keep up a strong gallop for more than a quarter mile. That's what the books say, and Ashleigh and the others always gallop the horses for a longer distance on the oval, even if they only go at a full-out gallop for a quarter or half mile." Cindy paused, her brow furrowed in thought. "We've only got about three more weeks. The Keeneland auction starts on January sixth, and the owners said they would pick Glory up a few days before that."

"It's getting that close?"

"Yup," Cindy replied grimly.

"How many more clockings do you think we'll need before he's ready?" Heather asked.

"Three at least. I've pretty much decided that I should talk to Sammy and see if she'll try him out."

"Do you think she will?" Heather asked. "I thought you didn't want to ask her to go behind her father's back."

"I know, but I don't know what else we can do. Sammy at least will understand why we've been secretly training him. She won't get angry with me, but I'm afraid my foster dad and Mike might be upset."

"But they're going to have to find out what we've been doing sometime."

"If Sammy will try Glory out, she can talk to the men. They trust her opinion, and it would be easier for her to convince them to breeze Glory on the track. I'm afraid they won't listen to what you and I have to say. They'll think we're too inexperienced to know."

"What if Sammy won't help?"

Cindy's jaw tightened. "We'll think of something. Let's canter."

"We'll probably drop behind after a few strides," Heather said, "but I don't mind chasing Glory."

The girls increased the pace and soon reached the spot where Cindy had galloped Glory a few days before.

"What I was thinking I'd do," Cindy explained as they slowed the horses to a walk, "is to start galloping him farther down the lane. I think I can guess how far another quarter mile would be. I know it won't be exact, but it should tell us something. I brought some orange tape to

141

mark the start of the quarter mile we measured the other day. I'll start him at a medium gallop about a quarter mile before that, which should be just past the storage shed. Then when we hit the orange tape, I'll breeze him."

Heather giggled. Cindy looked over, frowning. "You think that's crazy?"

"No," Heather said. "It just sounds kind of funny—you talking about breezing—like we know what we're doing."

"Well, we sort of know what we're doing," Cindy shot back, feeling offended. "We're trying, anyway!"

"I know," Heather said. "I'm sorry, but you sounded like Mike and Ian giving instructions to riders—so professional."

Cindy forgave her friend and smiled, seeing the humor. "Okay. I agree, but if we don't act professionally, we'll never get Glory anywhere."

"Right. I don't want Glory to go to auction and be sold to someone else."

Cindy swallowed hard. "And it's even more important to me." She pointed left along the intersecting lane. "I'll start him up there. This lane is straight. I think you'll be able to see me start."

Heather nodded. "With that red jacket you're wearing, I won't miss you."

Cindy rode Glory to the edge of the lane and stopped him at the corner of the fencing. She removed the yard of orange marker tape she had deposited in her parka pocket. She'd found it in the tack room. Every fall during hunting season, Len went out and marked all the outer fences of the property with the tape and No Hunting signs to warn hunters off the property. There was the ever present fear that hunters would mistake a horse for a deer—and some of the hunters who came into the area didn't know the difference. Vic had told them about the time he'd been in a nearby diner and had seen a goat strapped to the roof of a Jeep Cherokee with Maryland plates and heard the owner of the car bragging inside the diner about this great deer he'd shot. The state police had heard too, and quickly intervened to fine him and demand compensation to the goat's owners.

Cindy tied the tape around the rail so that it was clearly visible from the end of the quarter mile. "Here's what we'll do," she said. "I'll ride Glory up the lane by the shed. Hit the stopwatch when we start. I know it's not going to be accurate, but it's better than nothing. Then hit the watch again when we pass this orange tape at the beginning of the quarter mile, then again at the end. Do you know how to work that watch for several timings? I don't."

"Yeah," Heather said. "I'll get it right."

"Ready?"

"Here goes. Good luck!" Heather reined Bo to the right while Cindy reined Glory to the left and cantered up the lane, stopping at what she estimated to be a quarter mile. She turned Glory.

Far in the distance she saw Heather rein Bo in close to the fence and turn. Heather raised her hand and waved. Cindy guessed the gesture meant Heather could see them clearly.

Cindy prepared herself. Remembering their last gallop, when she had nearly lost her balance, Cindy had wrapped her fingers in Glory's mane. She was ready when Heather lifted and dropped her hand again. She immediately heeled Glory forward, crouching over his withers. The colt jumped out eagerly—almost too eagerly, and Cindy had to struggle to hold him to a moderate pace. Her arm muscles quivered with the effort needed to stop him from flattening out into a full gallop. Even with the firm pressure she was putting on the reins, Cindy knew they were going faster than she wanted.

Glory's long strides swept them forward. Cindy couldn't believe how quickly they were approaching the intersection of the lanes where the orange tape marked out the beginning of the quarter mile.

Her hands and arms were trembling as she continued trying to hold Glory to a moderate pace. She felt an instant's fear that she wouldn't be able to control him. In the next split second, she pushed the fear aside. Glory wasn't deliberately disobeying his rider. He just wanted to run . . . and run. This was what he loved. This was what he'd been born to do. Cindy had to content herself with being along for the ride.

They were two strides from the start tape, then one. As they flashed past, Cindy gave Glory the rein he wanted. He instantly switched to a higher gear. His gallop was so smooth, it seemed as if his feet weren't even touching the ground, that he was flying over it. *This is amazing*, Cindy thought, then forced her concentration to the task still ahead.

"Keep it up, boy. That's the way!"

Glory's ears were cocked back, listening to her voice,

but her encouragement wasn't really necessary. He was doing it all by himself.

They roared past Heather and Bo, and Cindy lifted her weight away from Glory's withers. After their last gallop, she was prepared and didn't panic when he was reluctant to slow down. She turned him in a large circle around the meadow. Perhaps because he had galloped over a longer distance that day, he responded to the pressure on his reins and by the end of the circle dropped back into a canter.

Cindy patted his neck. "That was wonderful, big guy! I'm so proud of you."

Glory arched his neck and pranced, and Cindy headed him back toward Heather and Bo.

Heather's eyes were so wide, Cindy chuckled. "I guess we were good," she called to her friend.

"I guess!" Heather said breathlessly. "I thought you said you were going to keep it slow for the first quarter."

"I was trying to, but he didn't want to listen."

"Well, I know you were only guessing at the distance, but he clocked the first quarter in twenty-four seconds . . . and the second in twenty-two."

Cindy beamed. "I knew it. It seemed like we were flying."

"You were. It felt like a wind tunnel when you went by us. Do you want to clock him again tomorrow?"

"Yes—that is, if he doesn't seem sore or anything."

"Two gallops like that should prove something," Heather said excitedly.

"I think so too, but I think we need a couple more

145

before we say anything to anyone . . . just to be sure. And we can't breeze him every time we go out. Ian and Mike never do with their horses, and the books say too many hard works can stress a horse."

"Maybe by Christmas he'll be ready," Heather said.

"Maybe," Cindy answered with a nod. She realized that she and Heather were far from experts at judging talent in a horse, but her eyes were sparkling.

Cindy was so excited about Glory that she found it hard not to burst out with her news at the dinner table that night. She had to bite her tongue when Ian started talking to Samantha about the horses he was bringing to Gulfstream in mid-January.

"It's really disappointing, but there isn't a star in the bunch. Rocky Heights always carries his weight in allowance races, but we just don't have any stakes-winning potential this year. That's where we need some strength. I'll be glad when Mr. Wonderful and Precocious start their two-year-old training. I think both of them have a huge amount of potential, but they won't start racing until late spring or summer."

"What about that colt Mike is training for an outside owner?" Beth asked. "I thought Mike was enthusiastic about him."

"Was. He put in some brilliant works early on, but he's inconsistent—a very moody animal."

Beth suddenly frowned in worry. "You don't think the farm's in trouble this season, do you?"

"No. Things are definitely not that bad," Ian said. "I guess we all got spoiled when we were racing big winners like Pride and Jazzman. Of course there's Shining, but Sammy is training her." He looked across the table to his daughter and smiled. "Mike and I can't take any credit for that."

"You've still got Blues King," Samantha said.

"But he won't be racing again until spring."

You could have Glory, Cindy thought, exchanging a quick look with Heather, then ducking her head to hide her expression from the others.

"It's not realistic to expect to have a big star every year, Ian," Beth said. "I know . . . I don't know that much about the business, but I've heard of other trainers having lean years."

Ian chuckled. "Hey, Sammy, we're teaching her, aren't we? I seem to remember at one point that Beth didn't know the front end of a horse from the back."

"Now, I'm not that stupid," Beth protested, but they all laughed, and she soon joined in.

Later, after they had gone out to say their good-nights to Glory and the other horses, Cindy and Heather huddled in Cindy's room and talked.

"It sounds better for Glory all the time," Heather said. "I thought Whitebrook always had a bunch of good horses racing. I was surprised to hear they didn't this year."

"Mmmm," Cindy murmured. "I didn't know that

either. I mean, I've watched a lot of workouts, but I've never heard Ian and Mike say the horses they have in training were duds."

"Do you think any of them have worked as fast as Glory?"

"Some of them have, I think, but you heard what Ian said about being inconsistent. So far, Glory isn't. He just keeps getting better."

"But will he keep doing that?" Heather asked worriedly.

Cindy wagged her head. "I don't know. I've never galloped any other racehorses, but I feel like Glory's really putting his heart into it. He loves running, and I just don't think that he'll stop loving it."

"I hope not."

They'd already changed into their nightgowns and were sitting cross-legged on Cindy's bed. Heather propped her elbows on her legs and cupped her chin with her hands. "Have you ever been to an auction?"

"Sort of," Cindy said. "When we were at Saratoga this summer, they had a big auction just when we got there. We didn't go, but I saw all the people who came and a lot of the horses that were being auctioned."

"Were the horses good-looking?"

"You bet. They were gorgeous."

"You don't know how much they went for?"

Cindy shook her head. "No, and I was thinking about other things. Shining and Blues King were both racing."

"So you've never been to a Keeneland auction."

"No, but I've been reading about them in the racing

magazines," Cindy said. "People come from all over the world to buy horses. Sammy told me that the Japanese, the Europeans, and the Arabs are all big buyers."

"So there will be people with a lot of money."

"And one of them could buy Glory and ship him out of this country. It's bad enough that he could be sold to someone here. But at least then we could hear about his races, maybe even watch them. If he goes to another country . . ." Cindy let the sentence hang as she stared into space.

"We'll do it, Cin. We'll prove to everyone that Whitebrook should buy him—that he'll be worth it."

Cindy didn't know how they would do it, but somehow they would.

14

Cindy's stomach was tied up in knots all day Tuesday, and she went into the interview with the child welfare people in semipanic. But it turned out better than she'd expected.

Ian and Beth were completely behind her and gave her strength, and the session was nothing like those that she'd been through before—different people, different circumstances. She didn't trust the child welfare people when the interview began, but by its end, she was feeling almost relaxed.

Their questions were quietly phrased. They weren't trying to find fault, like Mrs. Lovell had done. They listened when she told them how happy she was with Ian and Beth and at Whitebrook. They smiled when she talked about the horses and how much she loved working with them. They congratulated her on her report card. They weren't rude to Ian and Beth, either.

They asked about Beth's work with disabled children and remarked on Ian's success at raising Samantha alone after her mother's untimely death.

Still, Cindy was distrustful enough of all government authority figures that she wondered if their pleasantness was just a trick. She asked both her foster parents about it when they were driving back to Whitebrook.

"I don't think so, Cindy," Beth replied. "What do you think, Ian?"

"No. Everything seemed pretty straightforward. I think they agreed that Cindy is doing very well—that everything has improved for her since she left her last foster home. They certainly didn't seem to think our being in the horse-racing business was a problem."

"Like Mrs. Lovell did?" Cindy asked.

Beth turned to look at Cindy in the backseat. "All I can say about Mrs. Lovell is that she wasn't suited to her job. She didn't have an open mind. She was too quick to judge without evidence. It's a sorry thing that she's still working in child welfare. With her attitudes, she can only do more harm than good."

"It was like she had made up her mind before she heard anything I had to say," Cindy said. "She made me feel like I was trash . . . that I'd never be any good."

"But we know otherwise, don't we?" Ian said. "That's behind us now. You're a wonderful kid with a lot of brains and talent. I know you've been through some awful things, but you have to keep believing in yourself."

"I do," Cindy said.

"We do too," Beth told her.

At their words, Cindy thought of the secret she was keeping from them even then. She felt a heavy twinge of guilt. Beth and Ian were so wonderful. They trusted her, and here she was breaking all the rules by training Glory behind their backs. But Glory was important too. There was a time when you had to do what you thought was best, even if it put you at risk and others didn't think the same way you did.

"Do you think they'll approve my adoption?" Cindy asked. There was a nervous tremor in her voice that she tried to hide.

"Yes, Cindy," Ian said. "I think they'll approve it, although we probably won't know their final decision until spring. You do want to become our adopted daughter?"

"Yes," Cindy answered fervently. "Yes."

Cindy and Heather planned on timing Glory again that weekend. In the meantime, Cindy worked him on the longe line and walked him for miles over the trails in between. She cursed the fact that she couldn't ride him out alone, but she wasn't going to push the point by asking Ian or Mike. They would never let her ride out on a powerful horse without someone keeping her company in case something went wrong.

On Thursday afternoon, Cindy led Glory back into the stable after a long walk. As she passed the stable office, she heard Ian and Mike talking and stopped in her tracks when she heard what they were discussing.

"I just got a call from Skoglund," Mike said to Ian.

"They've changed their plans. They want to pick up Glory in the next couple of days. They've already rented stalls at Keeneland."

"I'm sorry to hear that," Ian said sadly. "It's not going to make Cindy happy."

"I feel bad for her," Mike agreed. "But I don't know what else we can do. Skoglund was firm about not considering an offer below ten thousand, and as much as we'd all like Cindy to keep the colt, we just can't afford that much for an untried horse."

"I know. We're really caught between a rock and a hard place. I'll talk to Cindy."

Cindy had to stop herself from bursting into Mike's office and shouting out that Glory wasn't unproven—he did have talent. She knew that would be a mistake. She had to think this through, even though the conversation had sent her heart plummeting to her feet.

She quickly led Glory to his stall. "I've got to talk to Heather," she said to the colt. "Then I'll be back to groom you." Latching his stall, she rushed to the cottage. No one was there, so she used the phone in the kitchen and quickly dialed Heather's number, praying that Heather would be home.

She answered on the third ring. "I just got awful news, Heather," Cindy cried breathlessly. "They're coming for Glory in a few days."

Heather gasped. "What? But the auction's not for two weeks."

"They've changed their plans. They're going to stable him at Keeneland."

"Oh, no, Cin. What are we going to do? You've got to talk to Sammy and ask her to help us. Do you think Glory's ready? We've only clocked two gallops."

"I don't know if he's ready or not, but we've run out of time. I'll try to talk to Sammy tonight, but I know she'll be home late. She's going somewhere with Tor."

"You sound like you don't think she'll help," Heather said.

"I think she may want to, but can she? I don't know if Mike and Ian will let even Sammy take Glory out on the oval."

"Then you ride him," Heather said. "Take him out during morning workouts before anyone can stop you."

"I've never ridden on the oval. I'm afraid I'd mess up."

"How much do you want Glory?" Heather asked.

Cindy hesitated, thinking about what could happen if she took matters in her own hands. She might be able to prove Glory's worth, but she knew without question the adults would be furious with her if she galloped the colt on the oval. She didn't have the experience to work a horse, especially one that didn't belong to the farm. But Glory's future was important too. She didn't want him sold to a stranger—maybe even shipped out of the country. How would she ever know whether he was being cared for and loved?

"Cin?" Heather questioned.

"What if I blow it and can't get him to run? I'll just be getting all of us in trouble and it won't help Glory one bit."

"You haven't blown his gallops yet," Heather argued. "He'd do anything for you, and you know it."

"Yes." Cindy swallowed. "Why don't I talk to Sammy first before we make any plans?"

"Let me know what she says."

"I will." When Cindy had hung up the phone, she stared off into space. If she had to do it, she could, but it would be better all around if Samantha would help them.

When she returned to the barn to groom Glory, she felt sick with indecision. Glory sensed something was wrong and blew soft breaths in her ear as if to reassure her. "I don't know what I'm going to do, boy. Actually I know what I have to do, but can I?"

She was interrupted by footsteps outside the stall. "Cindy?" her foster father called quietly.

"I'm here."

He stepped inside the stall. Cindy could tell from his expression that he wasn't happy about what he had to tell her. She made it easier for him.

"I heard you and Mike talking," she said in a choked voice. "They're coming for Glory in a few days."

He stepped over and put his arm around her shoulders. "I'm so sorry."

Cindy suddenly felt her eyes flood with tears. She blinked them away. "It's not your fault."

"No. I just wish they had accepted our offer."

"I know, but you tried."

Ian gave her a sad look. "I'm proud of you for being so brave."

Would he be so proud, Cindy wondered, if he knew what she and Heather were planning? She asked the question foremost on her mind. "Would the farm have been willing to pay more for him if he were trained and looked like he had talent?"

"Well, of course. But that's not the case, sweetheart. He's only had preliminary training, and no one knows whether he has talent or not."

Cindy was on the verge of admitting what she and Heather had been doing and how fast they'd clocked Glory, but she bit her tongue. She was afraid he'd be angry. She needed to talk to Samantha first. She couldn't take the chance of being forbidden to show Glory off.

Ian took her silence for pain. "There's always the chance that he won't bring what the estate expects, and they'll be open to lower offers."

Cindy nodded. Her throat felt so tight, she couldn't talk. She felt like she was drowning in lies and deceit, but she didn't see that she had any options.

"I'll let you finish your grooming," Ian said finally. "I'm sorry about the way it's turned out."

"I know. Thanks," Cindy murmured.

When Ian was gone, Cindy pressed her forehead against Glory's silky neck and heaved a misery-laden sigh.

Over dinner, Beth added her sympathies which didn't make Cindy feel any better. After she'd helped with the dishes, Cindy went up to her room, but she could barely concentrate on her homework. She fidgeted and felt nervous butterflies fluttering in her stomach as she waited for Samantha to come home.

When she finally heard the front door open and Samantha call hello to Ian and Beth, Cindy screwed up her courage. A moment later she heard Samantha's footsteps on the stairs. Cindy waited for her to get settled, then crossed the hall and knocked on Samantha's door.

"That you, Cindy? Come on in," Samantha called cheerfully. "You look like the sky has fallen," Samantha said when she got a good look at the younger girl. "What's wrong?"

Cindy explained about Glory being picked up in a few days.

"Oh, Cindy, I'm sorry."

"I wanted to talk to you about Glory," Cindy said in a rush. "Heather and I have been conditioning him—I know, we shouldn't have been, but I wanted to prove he was good. I thought Whitebrook would pay more for him if they knew. And he is good!" Cindy hesitated. She could see Samantha's kind but skeptical expression. "But now that he's only going to be here a few more days, I was hoping you could ride him and show Ian and Mike . . . "

Samantha was slowly shaking her head. "I can't, Cindy. I've already talked to Dad and Mike. It would be unethical for them to let me work Glory without the owner's permission. Their hands are tied. I don't mean to be cruel. I know how you feel, because I've felt that

157

way myself. I want you to be able to keep Glory, but things don't always go the way you'd like. Charlie used to tell me that. You remember me telling you about Charlie Burke, the old trainer who helped Ashleigh train Wonder and Pride?"

Cindy nodded.

"You have to think about the fact that Glory's been out of training for so long, too. No one would let me take out a horse who's out of condition."

"But Heather and I have been conditioning him!" Cindy cried. "He's in great shape!"

"Cindy," Samantha said gently. "You're smart and quick to learn, but neither you nor Heather has any experience training. How do you know the colt's in condition?"

"I've been reading the training books, and I've watched enough workouts."

"It takes years of working with horses to be able to know when a horse is in top shape. A few weeks of canters aren't going to do the trick."

"We galloped him too, Sammy. He's fast!"

Samantha's brows shot up. "Don't tell Dad or Mike that you galloped him," she said sternly. "Do you know how easily he could have been injured?"

"But he wasn't, and I was careful."

"Still, you were taking a huge risk—not only for yourself and Glory, but for Dad and Mike. How would they look if Glory had been hurt? The estate would hold them responsible." Samantha wagged her head. "And here everyone was thinking you and Heather were just trotting over the lanes. I'm not trying to lecture you, because at your age I might have done the same thing, but that doesn't mean what you did was right."

Cindy cringed at the criticism. She'd done the only thing she could to keep Glory. By now, Cindy knew that Samantha couldn't help them, even if she wanted to. Cindy could have argued that she was a better judge of Glory's talent than Samantha thought. She could have quoted Glory's clockings, but a seed of doubt was forming in her own mind. Maybe she was being naive and unrealistic. Maybe Glory's twenty-three-second quarter miles didn't mean a thing if he hadn't already been worked for over a mile.

She sighed and dropped her head.

"I know how tough this is for you, Cin," Samantha said. "But there's still the chance that he won't make his reserve at auction. Come here and let me give you a hug. It hurts me to see you feeling so down. I've been there."

Cindy stepped over to Samantha and was enveloped in a warm and caring hug. She knew how much Samantha empathized, but that wasn't going to keep Glory from being sold. It was up to her now.

15

"I'M SO NERVOUS, HEATHER," CINDY SAID AS THEY QUIETLY slipped out of her bedroom the next night. Cindy had decided that they needed to take Glory out to the oval so it would be familiar to him when she galloped him in the morning.

"I know," Heather responded. "I'm nervous too, but I think you're right. Glory needs to get used to the oval."

They edged down the stairs. The cottage was dark and quiet. Cindy cringed when a board creaked under her feet. It was midnight. Everyone at Whitebrook was long since in bed, as they would be up again so early in the morning.

The girls said nothing more until they were safely out of the cottage and crossing the stable yard. "At least we lucked out with the moon," Heather said, looking up at a cloudless sky and a bright three-quarter moon.

"There are some spotlights near the training oval, but

this is a lot better." Cindy's heart was pounding in her throat, but she was determined. "I'm just going to trot him around once," she told Heather in a whisper. "I'd like to canter him, but I don't want anyone to hear us."

"Len and Vic's cottage is far enough away from the oval that they shouldn't hear," Heather said reassuringly.

"We just have to be careful we don't wake up the other horses and start them whinnying. Len would be out here in a shot."

They slipped into the training barn, where night-lights burned dimly. On tiptoe, they made their way to Glory's stall. Cindy had hidden his tack in the trunk in the aisle after dinner. Heather collected it as Cindy carefully unlatched Glory's stall door.

The big gray snorted, surprised to be having visitors at this time of night. "Easy, boy," Cindy whispered, reaching out for his muzzle. "It's just me."

Imp rose from Glory's back and stretched sleepily.

Cindy continued whispering to the colt. "I know this isn't what you're used to, but it's important. It could make the difference between whether you stay here or not. Shhh, Glory. Don't wake up the other horses."

In the dim light, Cindy could see Glory's ears were pricked. He shifted uneasily, but remained quiet. Heather entered the stall with the tack.

"We're going out for a little ride, Glory." Cindy lifted a still sleepy Imp from the colt's back and removed Glory's blanket. As she buckled the saddle in place and put on Glory's bridle, Cindy realized her hands were trembling. She tried to steady them. She didn't want Glory to pick up on her nervousness and become nervous himself.

"I almost feel like a burglar," Heather whispered.

"Me too, but we're not. Have you got the booties?" Cindy asked. Heather handed her four cloth hoof covers that were sometimes used when horses were shipped. She was hoping the cloth would muffle the sound of Glory's iron-shod hooves as they walked down the concrete aisle and out of the barn.

"Ready?" she asked Heather.

"Let's go." Heather's answering tone was tight with worry.

Cindy slowly led Glory from his stall. The colt was obviously confused by the change in his normal schedule. He huffed and looked around. "It's okay, boy. Easy."

The cloth booties were working. Glory's hooves made barely a sound as they proceeded down the aisle and into the cold night air.

All was still quiet. Cindy removed the booties, led Glory to the mounting block, and got in his saddle, all the while trying to reassure him with her voice. She fastened the strap of her hard hat, then turned him toward the training oval sixty yards away.

Cindy tensed at every sound, but the windows of the main house and the two cottages remained dark. It seemed to take forever to cross the short distance to the track, but finally they reached the gap, the open spot where she and Glory could enter the mile oval.

Glory was fully awake now and looking around

curiously, flicking his ears back and forth. "It's okay, boy. There aren't any bad guys out there. We're just going to trot once around, okay?" Cindy asked softly.

She sensed that the only reason Glory willingly walked onto the oval was because of his trust in her. The moon cast enough light so that Cindy could see fairly clearly. Everything was bathed in a silvery white glow. Heather waited near the gap. Her face looked eerily pale in the moonlight.

Cindy circled Glory at a walk, loosening him up, then brought him close to the inside rail and asked him to trot. He did, but she felt his muscles quiver. He wasn't happy being out in the dark in unfamiliar territory. "It's okay, Glory. I know this is strange, but nothing's going to hurt you."

Glory snorted softly, but kept moving forward at a trot. Cindy kept him close to the inside rail, as she had seen Ashleigh and Samantha do. But as they came around the first turn, she was beginning to realize that the oval was a lot bigger than it seemed from the sidelines. She again felt a twinge of doubt about her knowledge and ability. Was she right about Glory's talent? Was she capable of galloping him around the ring later that morning and proving it to the others?

Cindy shook the thought away. She couldn't start doubting herself now or she would never have the courage to do what she had to do. More important, she couldn't let Glory down.

By the time they passed the half-mile marker, Glory actually seemed to be relaxing. Cindy tried to relax too—to forget the trials that would come in the morning and just enjoy this ride in the moonlight with the horse she loved.

As they rounded the far turn, she focused her eyes straight ahead and asked Glory to pick up his trot. *Not much farther*, she thought. She could see Heather just ahead. Cindy held the colt in close to the rail while they finished the full circuit of the oval. Then, praising Glory, she slowed him and turned back to the gap.

She was amazed at how relieved she felt that it was over. If she felt like this after a trot, how was she going to gallop Glory over this same track in less than six hours?

Heather was waiting as Cindy rode Glory off the track. "It looked good," Heather said. "He didn't seem spooked or anything."

"No, he was okay. It's me I'm worried about. Heather, I don't know if I can do it."

"Yes, you can," Heather whispered defiantly. "I've seen you ride him on the lanes. You can do the same tomorrow on the oval."

Quietly they moved across toward the barns. They were halfway there when a light in Len and Vic's cottage suddenly went on. Both of them froze.

"They've heard us!" Cindy murmured anxiously.

"Don't move," Heather said.

They both watched the cottage, but the front door didn't open. Except for the light, all was quiet.

"Let's go," Cindy said. "The sooner we have him back in his stall, the better."

They moved forward again. Cindy's heart didn't stop pounding until they had Glory settled, with his gear back in the tack room, and were slipping across the stable yard to the cottage.

They let themselves in and gingerly climbed the stairs. When they reached Cindy's room, they eased the door shut, then collapsed on the bed.

"We did it," Heather said.

Yes, Cindy thought, but the real test would come in less than six hours.

Cindy was jarred awake by the alarm clock. She'd been dreaming that she was out on a training track, and she couldn't get her horse to move. Something frightening was approaching, but the horse refused to budge. Cindy was at the point of jumping off his back and running to safety herself, but she didn't want to leave the horse to a horrible fate.

As Cindy turned off the alarm and threw her legs over the side of the bed, she felt uneasy, even though she knew it had only been a dream.

"The workouts start at six?" Heather asked groggily as she climbed from her sleeping bag. Since there was only a single bed in the room, Heather always brought her sleeping bag and slept on the rug on the floor.

"Yes. It depends on the light. The days are getting shorter, so sometimes they don't start until six thirty."

"We'd better get going, then," Heather said. "You've got to warm up Glory."

Cindy was suddenly fully alert. Her throat felt tight as she reached for her clothes. She could always back out, she told herself. She didn't have to take Glory on the oval. But then she would be letting Glory down— giving up without a fight.

Within minutes the girls were out in the stable. With Heather's help, Cindy hurried through her chores, trying not to think of what was ahead. The others came into the barn, calling greetings and setting to work.

Ian called to Vic, asking the groom to tack up the first of the horses he'd be working. Mike wouldn't be working any horses that morning, and he busied himself in his office.

When Ian, Vic, and Samantha had left the barn for the oval, Cindy went and collected Glory's tack. She was so nervous that Heather had to help her with the buckles on the girth and bridle.

Cindy had carefully planned what she would do. First she would take Glory out to the lane on the far side of the mares' barn and warm him up. They would be out of sight of the oval there. When the colt was warmed up, Cindy would ride him around behind the barns, where they would still be out of view from the oval. The horses that were being worked were brought in and out through the front of the barn.

Heather walked beside Cindy as she headed Glory out to the lane. The colt was perky and bright and glad to be outside. He put an energetic prance in his strides. Heather leaned against the fence while Cindy trotted Glory up the lane.

It's going to be all right, Cindy told herself over and over. *We're going to do it. I'm not going to think about anything bad happening.*

Farther up the lane, she urged Glory into a canter and rode him up and down the lane until she was sure he was warmed up and limber. Then she rode back to Heather.

"You look as white as a ghost," Heather said with concern.

"That's because I'm scared."

"That you'll get in trouble?"

"Or that I'll mess up," Cindy said.

"You won't. You never have before. Pretend that you're just out galloping on the trails."

Cindy took a deep breath and squared her shoulders. "This is it, I guess. Let's go before I get any more nervous."

They walked off the lane and behind the barns. Suddenly Len stepped out from the side of one of the stable buildings. Cindy saw the puzzled look on his face and froze. She knew he had to be wondering what she was doing riding Glory so early in the morning. Her heart pounded as she waited for Len to say something. They had gotten this far; she didn't want anything to stop them now. But Len just lifted a hand in greeting and strode off toward the stallion barn.

"Whew!" Cindy sighed.

"I know," Heather agreed. "I was sure he was going to ask us what we were doing out here this early."

Cindy urged Glory forward again. Her head felt like it was stuffed with cotton. She was so nervous, she couldn't think straight. But they had reached the corner of the training barn, and ahead she saw the oval.

Only Vic and Ian were standing at the rail, watching Samantha work one of the horses.

"As soon as Sammy rides off," Heather whispered, "you should probably get him right out there."

Cindy nodded. Samantha finished her work and trotted her mount off the track and along the rail to where Ian and Vic were standing. None of them had seen the girls. Cindy knew that this was her chance. She had to get Glory onto the oval while none of them were looking. "Here goes," she murmured to Heather.

"Good luck!"

Cindy heeled Glory into a canter. His long strides quickly carried them across the ground to the oval. Cindy didn't pause, but urged him through the gap onto the track. She was on automatic pilot now, concerned only with getting through the gallop in one piece.

She reined Glory in toward the rail and continued cantering up the track. She didn't dare think about Ian and Sammy's reactions to seeing her out on the oval. At the three-quarter pole, Cindy urged Glory into a slow gallop. She had already decided that she would wait until the half before asking him to really dig in.

They entered the turn. As they neared the three-quarter pole, Cindy dropped lower over Glory's withers and gave him rein. He instantly changed stride, moving out in a moderate gallop, yet Cindy sensed the colt was uneasy. He wasn't concentrating as he normally did. Had he picked up on her nervousness?

Cindy tried to relax and sharpen her own concentration, but she felt numb. Her hands and legs suddenly felt like rubber, refusing to do what she wanted them to do. This was nothing like galloping on the lanes. She had to be crazy to even think about doing this.

Her weak signals were confusing Glory. His normally fluid strides were uneven. The half-mile marker was just ahead. She felt Glory begin to break stride. She forced her legs against his girth, but knew immediately that she'd used too much pressure. Glory, totally unsettled now, lunged forward into a full gallop, nearly unseating Cindy. She grabbed onto his mane, feeling growing panic. She was losing control of the colt.

The oval ahead seemed endless as Cindy clutched mane and reins and strove to stay balanced over the galloping colt's withers. Glory continued plunging forward. *I'm sure not doing Glory any good by this ride,* Cindy thought, fear rising in her throat. *I've blown it.*

She had to pull him up before he hurt himself. It was an admission of failure, but Cindy knew she had no choice.

She tried to sit straighter in the saddle and lean her weight away from Glory's neck. She pulled back on the reins. "Whoa, boy, whoa. Slow down!" Cindy heard the quiver of panic in her voice and knew Glory heard it too.

The colt didn't respond. He continued galloping headlong. *He's running away with me—and it's all my fault!*

169

Cindy put more pressure on the reins and still got no response from the colt. "Please, Glory. Whoa!"

They pounded off the far turn. Ahead she saw Samantha and Ian out on the track, both looking frightened. Glory saw them too, and finally he began to shorten his stride. Cindy stood higher in the stirrups and continued her pressure on the reins.

After a few more strides Glory dropped back into a canter, then a trot. Cindy was shaking like a leaf when she stopped him. Samantha rushed toward them. She took Glory's head and soothed the colt.

"I'm so sorry," Cindy cried, near tears. "I wanted to show everyone how good he was . . . I didn't want to lose him . . . but I've only made things worse."

"Are you all right?" Samantha asked worriedly.

Cindy nodded.

"Then dismount and hold him."

Cindy's legs were trembling so badly, she nearly fell out of the saddle. She took Glory's reins from Samantha and watched in disbelief as Samantha quickly got up into the saddle.

"What are you doing?"

"I think he has talent too, and I'm going to help you prove it. I'll take him around."

Ian raced up. His expression was such a mixture of emotions, Cindy didn't know what to think, but she was sure there would be some angry words.

Just as he reached their side, Samantha heeled Glory off up the track.

"Sammy!" Ian shouted. "What are you doing?"

170

"Showing off your next wonder horse," she called back over her shoulder.

"That's not our horse!" her father cried, but Samantha was already cantering away. "Come on," Ian said to Cindy, taking her arm. "Do you know what kind of a risk you just took? What were you thinking of?"

"I wanted to prove he was good," Cindy said in trembling tones. "So we could keep him."

"And what is Sammy thinking of?" Ian continued angrily, staring up the track at his daughter. "She of all people should know better than to gallop an unconditioned horse!"

"He is conditioned," Cindy said weakly. "Heather and I have been working him."

"You? Working him how?"

"First long walks and trots, then canters. Then we clocked him twice at a gallop."

Ian groaned, but hurried them off the track. "You have a lot of explaining to do, young lady."

"I know . . . but will you watch the workout first?"

He was already looking in that direction. Samantha had Glory galloping smoothly down the backstretch. Out of habit, Ian reached for his stopwatch and clicked it as Samantha and Glory reached the half-mile pole.

Heather joined Cindy at the rail, but they all remained silent while they watched the rest of the workout.

Samantha had picked up the pace, but not until they reached the quarter pole did she start Glory breezing. He shot forward, his long strides making the pace seem effortless.

"Wow," Vic muttered under his breath. Cindy glanced over to her foster father. His eyes were glued to the colt. Glory and Samantha pounded past, heading toward the wire. As they swept by, Samantha rose in the stirrups and began slowing the colt.

Vic gave a low whistle, then said to Ian, "Was it my imagination, or was that colt burning up the track?"

"It wasn't your imagination," Ian said, glancing at his watch. There was disbelief in his voice. "I clocked the quarter in twenty-two, and he didn't even look like he was trying."

Cindy's knees shook with relief. She grabbed onto the rail to steady herself.

"Looks like you've got something here," Vic murmured.

"I never would have guessed he had this kind of talent," Ian said, then turned to the girls and spoke sternly. "That's not to say I approve of what you two did. The results could just as easily have been disastrous."

"I know," Cindy agreed meekly. "But we didn't know what else to do."

Samantha rode up, smiling broadly, and Cindy hurried over. She took Glory's head and kissed his nose. "You were super, boy! I love you!"

Ian strode over and looked up at his daughter. "I should be furious with you, Sammy."

Samantha didn't look the least bit dismayed. "I know, Dad, but you aren't. I knew Cindy and Heather had been conditioning him."

"And you didn't say anything?"

"Cindy only told me two days ago. And before you ask, I didn't know Cindy intended to take him on the track."

Ian was scowling.

"Look at the bright side," Vic said. "You've found a horse with talent, and he's for sale."

Samantha dismounted, and Ian carefully inspected Glory, feeling each of his legs, walking him in a circle to check for any signs of soreness. Finally he said to Vic, "Cool him out, then check his legs again. You girls come with me."

He strode off in the direction of the training stable. The girls exchanged a puzzled look but followed.

"Don't worry," Samantha said with a smile. "I'll bet you anything that Dad's going to talk to Mike about upping their offer."

"To ten thousand?" Cindy asked.

"I think he's worth it now."

Mike and Ian were talking earnestly when the girls entered the office.

Mike's brow was furrowed. "Sure it's not a fluke?"

"Cindy tells me they've worked him before."

"Both workouts were under twenty-three seconds for the quarter," Cindy put in.

Mike looked at Cindy and lifted his brows. There was a hint of a smile on his lips. "Well, I trust your judgment, Ian, and our stable's not exactly overrun with talent this winter. Let's see if we can get Skoglund on the phone." Mike picked up the receiver.

Cindy looked over to Heather. She could barely believe what she was hearing. It had worked! Mike and Ian were going to buy Glory! She felt like she was going to faint from happiness. Heather looked just as pleasantly stunned.

Mike had Skoglund on the phone. "We're prepared to improve our offer on the colt and pay what you're asking," Mike said. There was a pause. "What? When was this decided? Our offer's firm. Why take an unnecessary chance at auction? Yes, yes. I see. All right, but I think you're making a mistake."

Mike put down the phone. He was frowning. "Skoglund says they're not considering further private offers for any of the stock. Since his office will be closed the next two weeks for the holiday, they're holding the stock for the auction."

"That's crazy," Ian said. "He could close the sale now."

"Actually, he can't. He's leaving for the airport in an hour for a trip with his family. They won't be back until after the new year."

"And no one in his office can handle the sale in his absence?"

"No one will be there. It's a small office. He's given all his staff the time off. He's hired a van to pick up Glory on Monday and bring him to Keeneland."

Cindy was devastated as she looked back and forth between the two men.

"I guess we'll just have to wait for the auction," Mike said, "and hope no one outbids us."

16

Cindy woke from a restless sleep the morning of January 6. It was auction day, and by that afternoon she would know for certain if Glory would return to Whitebrook.

The past two weeks had been an agony for Cindy. Just when she'd thought that Glory would definitely stay at Whitebrook, her dreams had been dashed, and once again there was no certainty about the colt's future.

She knew all hope wasn't lost. Mike would be bidding on Glory at the auction, but there were no guarantees that he would be the highest bidder. There would be wealthy buyers who might be willing to take a chance on an unraced colt at a price higher than Whitebrook could afford.

Even the Christmas festivities hadn't lightened her fearful mood. The Pony Commando show had been a huge success, and on Christmas morning she had opened her presents to discover a new pair of riding boots with leather as soft as butter. There'd been new riding clothes too, several books with color photos about raising and training horses, and a beautiful sweater for school.

She had been so very grateful for the gifts and the loving thoughtfulness behind them, but since the Monday morning when the van had come for Glory, she had been numb. She hadn't even been there to say goodbye. The van had come while she was in school, and she returned home to find Glory gone.

She missed him so much. She felt an aching emptiness inside every time she passed the stall that had been his. Imp seemed lost too, with his buddy gone.

During vacation week, Heather had come over nearly every day. Cindy knew she could have borrowed another of the exercise horses and gone riding, but she couldn't face the thought of going out on the lanes and being reminded of her rides and gallops on Glory. Was he being treated well? Did he miss her as much as she missed him? Was he bewildered by his new surroundings—frightened? Was he beginning to mistrust humans again because they couldn't be depended on? Cindy hadn't even been able to visit the colt.

Cindy barely touched her breakfast and was tensely quiet as she, Ian, and Beth prepared to leave for the auction.

"I know how you're feeling," Ian said, "but remember, we have one very big advantage. We're the only ones who know the colt has talent. Other buyers will think they're bidding on an untried animal and won't be willing to go as high as we feel justified in doing."

"Do you know how high Mike is willing to bid?" Cindy asked tightly.

"We've already agreed to go to ten thousand, and frankly, I think that will be enough to get him."

"What if it's not?"

Ian hesitated. "I'm not sure. The farm has its limits financially. The decision will have to be Mike's. I'm only an employee, remember, and I've already put in all the money I can toward the purchase."

"Oh," Cindy murmured.

"There's nothing to be gained by thinking the worst, Cindy," Beth said encouragingly. "I think the odds are on our side."

Heather was in a quiet mood too when they picked her up. Neither girl had much to say until Ian pulled into the Keeneland parking lot. "Not as crowded as I thought," he said, "but it's early yet. I told Mike and Ashleigh and Sammy and Tor that we'd meet them by the auction ring. Let's go."

He led them through a gate to the backside barn area. Since there was no winter racing at Keeneland, the barns that normally housed racing Thoroughbreds now housed the horses to be auctioned. All Cindy wanted to do was find Glory.

Ian and Mike had gotten copies of the auction program days before and had carefully gone through pedigrees and history, looking for horses with potential.

Of course, there were plenty of other buyers who would be interested in the same animals.

They found the others and quickly joined them. "Have you had a chance to look around at all?" Ian asked Mike.

"No, we were waiting for you. It seems quiet so far."

"I hope it lasts. The fewer bidders, the better. The colt's in barn six."

The men led the way. Both of them knew the barn area at Keeneland like the palms of their hands.

Ashleigh stepped over to Cindy and smiled reassuringly. "Don't worry. Mike will get him."

"Are you sure?" Heather asked.

"As sure as I can be before the bidding starts."

Samantha put her hand on Cindy's shoulder. "He's going to be glad to see you."

At that Cindy smiled, picturing the big gray, imagining his nicker of greeting.

"The horses are so gorgeous," Heather said, looking around with wide eyes. "And there are so many of them."

"It's a big auction," Tor agreed.

Heather looked up at him. "Are you going to bid on any horses?"

"If something comes along that looks like a steal, I might." He grinned. "I have the advantage here, since I'm more interested in horses who don't look like good racing prospects but might be excellent jumpers."

Cindy had been looking around too, and she was just as awed as Heather at the quality of the horses. She hadn't thought the auction would be so huge. More people were arriving, too—most of them looking very serious and professional, with clipboards and programs in hand. She saw several Japanese in business suits, and an Arab in flowing robes. She heard foreign accents, local accents, and accents from other parts of the country. Her stomach tightened to think that any one of these people could be bidding on Glory.

"Down here," Ian said, leading them between two of the barns.

Cindy hurried after her foster father, but she didn't immediately see Glory. Prospective buyers stood in front of stalls, and grooms brought out horses for closer inspection. Then she saw him, near the end on the right. His head was over the stall door.

She quickened her steps and called out his name. "Glory!"

The big colt started. His head came up, and his ears pricked. He looked in the direction of her voice.

"I'm here, boy," she cried above the din of voices around her.

Glory bobbed his head, then let out a piercing whinny. Heads turned to look at the colt as Cindy rushed up to his stall. The colt was almost beside himself with happiness. He nickered and bobbed his head and made welcoming sounds in his throat when she reached his stall. He pressed his muzzle into Cindy's chest as she rubbed his ears and kissed his nose.

"I've missed you, boy. I've missed you so much!" Cindy felt tears sting her eyes. She was oblivious to the people who had turned to stare. "Have they been treating you okay?" Cindy asked. "You didn't think I deserted you, did you? Because I didn't. I didn't want anyone to take you away."

A groom stepped over and spoke in warning tones. "Watch it with that colt. He's a biter."

Cindy ignored the groom and smiled at Glory. "So you've been biting them, have you, boy? Good for you."

"Get back," the groom ordered. "This horse is in my charge, and I don't want to be responsible if you get hurt."

The rest of the Whitebrook group reached the stall, and Cindy heard her foster father's voice. "I can promise you he won't bite my daughter, since she's been his groom. The colt has been boarded with us at Whitebrook."

For an instant the groom glared, then he shrugged. "Only doing my job."

"I'm not trying to fault you—just to explain. We'd like to see the colt."

The groom nodded and took Glory's lead shank off its hook. Cindy stepped back as he unlatched the stall door and clipped the lead to Glory's halter, then led him out. "I only warned you because he's been a troublemaker," the groom said. "His temperament doesn't match his good looks. He happily takes a chunk out of anyone who doesn't know how to handle him."

Cindy barely heard his words. Her eyes were on Glory, inspecting every inch of him to see if he looked fit and well fed. Fortunately he did. Glory strained his head toward Cindy as the groom led him in a circle.

"Are you connected with that lawyer who's been coming around the last few days?" the groom asked curiously.

"We're not connected. We're interested buyers," Mike said.

Cindy suddenly noticed how many other buyers standing in the aisle were taking an interest in Glory, nodding and whispering to each other. She felt a chill. She didn't want other buyers getting interested in Glory and competing against Mike during the auction.

Mike had noticed too. "Well, thanks for bringing him out. We'll see. Beautiful horses don't necessarily make good runners. We've got some other horses to look at."

Cindy felt torn at leaving Glory. This might be the last chance she had to spend time with him. Glory looked at her as she departed, and he whickered repeatedly. Cindy saw the confusion in the colt's eyes. She tried to send him a silent message. *I'll be back, boy. We're trying to bring you back to Whitebrook.* She blew the colt a kiss, then turned and hurried after the others.

The crowd continued to increase. Cindy's stomach was in knots. She barely noticed the other horses Mike and Ian checked out. When the others went to get something to eat, she and Heather slipped back to barn 6 and watched Glory's stall from a distance.

During the ten minutes they watched, a half a dozen people asked the groom to bring Glory out. "Too many people are interested in him," she said miserably.

"He is beautiful," Heather said.

"I know, but right now I wish he were ugly and that

no one wanted to see him. Then no one else would bid on him."

"But there are so many other gorgeous horses here, Cin," Heather said. "And a lot of them have already raced."

"I know, I know."

She felt even more uneasy when they entered the auction ring a half hour later and the first horses were brought in. Every seat was taken, and people were standing in the aisles. Since it was a mixed sale, horses of all ages would be auctioned—yearlings, two-year-olds in training, older racing horses, broodmares.

Cindy stared toward the dirt ring as horse after horse was brought in and walked in front of the crowd. Each had a numbered tag attached to their hindquarters—a hip tag. Glory would be hip 102.

The bidding seemed to be going fast, but Cindy had no way of knowing if that was normal. She studied the horses as they were brought in. The prices paid varied drastically. Several horses weren't bid up to their reserves and were taken from the ring unsold. Other well-blooded, well-conformed yearlings and broodmares were bid up into the hundreds of thousands.

She gasped in disbelief when the bidding on a yearling colt out of Seattle Slew and Ruby's Red Slippers sold at over a million dollars to a Japanese buyer.

"A million dollars," Heather whispered to Cindy. "I don't believe it. How can any horse be worth that much?"

"Pride is," Cindy said, "and probably Jazzman is too."

"But that horse was a yearling. He hasn't even started training!"

Cindy grimaced and worried all the more about how high the bidding would go on Glory. She kept glancing at her program, wondering how long it would be before Glory would be brought into the ring and paraded in front of the auctioneer's stand.

Several more horses brought bids of over a hundred thousand dollars. Cindy was so tense, her palms were sweating. Then it was Glory's turn.

Misbehave, she silently told him. *Make yourself look as bad as you can so no one will bid on you but us.*

Glory seemed to be following her mental orders. He came into the ring, took one look at the huge crowd, and snorted, throwing up his head, eyeing the crowd uncertainly, trying to back away from his attendant. But even so, Cindy could see how gorgeous he looked. She heard the buzz of the crowd around her as they studied the colt. She looked around the audience and saw their quickened interest.

The auctioneer began. "So what am I bid on this fine three-year-old out of Great Beyond? Never been raced, but look at him—look at those hindquarters—look at that intelligent head. Let's start the bidding at five—five thousand for this handsome colt."

"Four thousand," someone called.

She looked over to Mike. He hadn't moved.

"I have four," the auctioneer chanted. "Who'll make it five . . . do I hear five? Thank you . . . now six . . . a bargain . . . do I hear six? Six it is!"

183

Mike had yet to bid, but he must know what he was doing, Cindy thought. He'd been to dozens of auctions before.

"Now I have seven . . . who'll make it eight?"

Cindy searched the crowd, trying to identify the bidders, but their signals to the auctioneer were so subtle, it was hard to tell.

Then she saw a Japanese businessman nod to the auctioneer.

"I have eight . . . who'll make it nine?"

Glory pranced at the end of his lead. Cindy turned to Mike. When was he going to bid? They'd almost reached ten thousand already. Then she saw him lift his program.

"I have new interest at nine . . . who'll make it ten . . . nine and a half . . . now ten."

Mike nodded.

"How about ten and a half . . . do I hear ten and a half?"

Cindy saw a man in the front row lift a finger.

The auctioneer looked in Mike's direction. "Eleven to you, sir."

Cindy's stomach clenched. They were already over ten thousand. How high would Mike go? *Please, Mike, go higher,* she silently pleaded.

Mike nodded, and Cindy gasped with relief.

But the other bidder wasn't ready to give up. He went to eleven fifty. Cindy couldn't breathe. She stared at Mike. He seemed to be making a decision. Finally he nodded.

"I have twelve . . . twelve to you, sir . . . "

Cindy glued her eyes to the man in the front row,

terrified he would raise the bid, because she had a horrible feeling that Mike had reached his limit.

Finally the man wagged his head. "All done at twelve?" the auctioneer cried. "Are there any more bids . . . final call . . ." He banged his gavel. "Sold to the gentleman." Mike held up his card. "Number forty-four."

For a moment Cindy sat stunned. Glory was theirs. He was coming back to Whitebrook. Then she felt a hand on her shoulder and heard Ian's cheerful voice. "What are you waiting for, Cindy? Let's go get our horse."

Cindy turned to him, a beaming smile on her face. Then she rose and went to Mike and hugged him. "Thank you . . . thank you so much!"

He grinned back. "I think I've made a wise investment."

Ian led the way as he, Beth, Cindy, and Heather hurried from the ring. Glory was being held by an attendant outside and was pacing uneasily. Cindy rushed toward the colt, calling his name. As soon as Glory saw her, he ceased his pacing and gave a loud and piercing whinny. Cindy had tears of joy in her eyes when she reached Glory's side and threw her arms around his neck.

"You're ours, boy—ours! You're going home to Whitebrook!"

Glory nuzzled her hair and whickered.

"Everything's going to be wonderful from now on. I love you, big guy, and soon you're going to be a great racehorse."

Glory gave a throaty nicker as if to say, "I know."

■ HarperPaperbacks *By Mail*

Ashleigh's Diary

THOROUGHBRED

Ashleigh's Christmas Miracle

Two Super Editions Now Available!

Read all the books in the Thoroughbred series and experience the thrill of riding and racing, along with Ashleigh Griffen, Samantha McLean, and their beloved horses.

MAIL TO: **■** HarperCollins*Publishers*
         P.O. Box 588 Dunmore, PA 18512-0588

Yes! Please send me the books I have checked:

❏ **#1 A HORSE CALLED WONDER** 106120-4 . . . . $3.50 U.S./$4.50 CAN.
❏ **#2 WONDER'S PROMISE** 106085-2. . . . . $3.50 U.S./$4.50 CAN.
❏ **#3 WONDER'S FIRST RACE** 106082-8. . . . .$3.50 U.S./$4.50 CAN.
❏ **#4 WONDER'S VICTORY** 106083-6 . . . .$3.50 U.S./$4.50 CAN.
❏ **#5 ASHLEIGH'S DREAM** 106737-7 . . . . $3.50 U.S./$4.50 CAN.
❏ **#6 WONDER'S YEARLING** 106747-4. . . . . $3.50 U.S./$4.50 CAN.
❏ **#7 SAMANTHA'S PRIDE** 106163-8. . . . . $3.50 U.S./$4.50 CAN.
❏ **#8 SIERRA'S STEEPLECHASE** 106164-6 . . . .$3.50 U.S./$4.50 CAN.
❏ **#9 PRIDE'S CHALLENGE** 106207-3 . . . . $3.50 U.S./$4.50 CAN.
❏ **#10 PRIDE'S LAST RACE** 106765-2 . . . . $3.50 U.S./$4.50 CAN.
❏ **#11 WONDER'S SISTER** 106250-2 . . . . $3.50 U.S./$4.50 CAN.
❏ **#12 SHINING'S ORPHAN** 106281-2. . . . .$3.50 U.S./$4.50 CAN.
❏ **#13 CINDY'S RUNAWAY COLT** 106303-7. . . . . $3.50 U.S./$4.50 CAN.
❏ **#14 CINDY'S GLORY** 106325-8. $3.50 U.S./$4.50 CAN.
❏ **ASHLEIGH'S CHRISTMAS MIRACLE*** 106249-9. . . . . . . $3.99 U.S./$4.99 CAN.
❏ **ASHLEIGH'S DIARY*** 106292-8 . . . . $3.99 U.S./$4.99 CAN.
*super edition

SUBTOTAL . . . .$_____
POSTAGE AND HANDLING . . . .$_____
SALES TAX (Add applicable sales tax) . . . .$_____
TOTAL . . . .$_____
Name_____
Address_____
City_____ State_____ Zip_____

Order 4 or more titles and postage & handling is **FREE!** Orders of less than 4 books please include $2.00
postage & handling. Remit in U.S. funds. Do not send cash. (Valid only in U.S. & Canada.)
Allow 6 weeks for delivery. Prices subject to change.   H11211

Visa & Mastercard holders—call 1-800-331-3761 for immediate service!

HarperPaperbacks *By Mail*

**This collection of spine-tingling horrors will scare you silly!
Be sure not to miss any of these eerie tales.**

BONE CHILLERS

#1: BEWARE THE SHOPPING MALL

Robin has heard weird things about Wonderland Mall. She's heard it's haunted. When she and her friends go shopping there, she knows something creepy is watching. Something that's been dead for a long, long time.

#2: LITTLE PET SHOP OF HORRORS

Cassie will do anything for a puppy. She'll even spend the night alone in a spooky old pet shop. But Cassie doesn't know that the shop's weird owner has a surprise for her. She can play with the puppies as long as she wants. She can stay in the pet shop . . . forever!

#3: BACK TO SCHOOL

Fitzgerald Traflon III hates the food at Maple Grove Middle School—it's totally gross. Then Miss Buggy takes over the cateferia, and things start to change. Fitz's friends love Miss Buggy's cooking, but Fitz still won't eat it. Soon his friends are acting really strange. And the more they eat . . . the weirder they get!

#4: FRANKENTURKEY

Kyle and Annie want to celebrate Thanksgiving like the Pilgrims. Then they meet Frankenturkey! Frankenturkey is big. Frankenturkey is bad. If Kyle and Annie don't watch out, Frankenturkey will eat *them* for Thanksgiving dinner.

#5: STRANGE BREW

Tori is bored stiff. Then she finds a mysterous notebook. Each time she opens it, a new spell appears. And each time she tries a spell, strange things happen. *Now* Tori's having fun . . . until the goofy spells turn gruesome.

#6: TEACHER CREATURE

Something is different about Joey and Nate's new teacher. His eyes bulge out, and his tongue is long and slimy. But all the kids like Mr. Batrachian—all except Joey and Nate who know the truth about him—sixth-graders are his favorite snack.

#7: FRANKENTURKEY II

When Kyle and Annie make wishes on Frankenturkey's wishbone from last year's Thanksgiving dinner, they bring him back to life. And this time, he wants revenge.

#8: WELCOME TO ALIEN INN*

When Matt's family stops at a roadside inn for the night, they don't realize that the innkeepers are aliens eager to experiment on the first Earthlings that come their way.

*coming soon

MAIL TO: **HarperCollins***Publishers*
P.O. Box 588 Dunmore, PA 18512-0588
OR CALL: (800) 331-3761

Yes, please send me the books I have checked:

❑ **Beware the Shopping Mall** 106176-X . .$3.50 U.S./$4.50 CAN.
❑ **Little Pet Shop of Horrors** 106206-5 . ..$3.50 U.S./$4.50 CAN.
❑ **Back to School** 106186-7 . . . .$3.50 U.S./$4.50 CAN.
❑ **Frankenturkey** 106197-2. . . . .$3.50 U.S./$4.50 CAN.
❑ **Strange Brew** 106299-5 . . . .$3.50 U.S./$4.50 CAN.
❑ **Teacher Creature** 106314-2 . . . .$3.50 U.S./$4.50 CAN.
❑ **Frankenturkey II** 106319-3 . . . .$3.50 U.S./$4.50 CAN.
❑ **Welcome to Alien Inn** 106320-7 . . . .$3.50 U.S./$4.50 CAN.

SUBTOTAL . . . .$_____
POSTAGE AND HANDLING . . . .$_____2.00____
SALES TAX (Add applicable sales tax). $_____
TOTAL . . . .$_____

Name_____

Address_____

City_____State_____Zip_____

Allow up to 6 weeks for delivery. Remit in U.S. funds. Do not send cash.
(Valid in U.S. & Canada.) Prices subject to change.   H10811

**Visa & Mastercard holders for fastest service call
1-800-331-3761**